PATH TO VILLAINY

An NPC Kobold's Tale

S.L. ROWLAND

ALSO BY S.L. ROWLAND

Sentenced to Troll

Sentenced to Troll 2

Sentenced to Troll 3

Pangea Online: Death and Axes

Pangea Online: Magic and Mayhem

Vestiges: Portal to The Apocalypse

For Scotty, thanks for being a part of the process.

CHAPTER ONE

"Greetings, adventurers! How may I assist you today?" Witt stared at the three armored heroes standing in front of him along the path to the Forgotten Quarters Dungeon.

A small gnome warrior stepped forward. He wasn't much bigger than Witt. Behind him, a minotaur mage and a human paladin watched with interest. The heroes were explorers from other worlds that appeared on the planet to go on quests, slay monsters, and increase their power.

The gnome was clad in shimmering mail that swallowed him whole. He had bright-green hair, and pointy ears. In one hand, he carried a sword as tall as he was. In the other, a small shield. "We would like to be buffed with one of your songs so that we may defeat the nearby dungeon."

Witt extended his hand. "Five silver."

After the gnome reached into his pouch and handed over the five silver coins, Witt took his lute and gently stroked the strings. Their tender melody filled the air, and a soft glow formed around the warrior and his party.

Witt softly sang a tune.

"It was a day, a normal day, when Scrabolt became aware,

that deep within the mountain's caves, there lived a mighty bear.
The bear was strong and hardy, but Scrabolt was as well.
He gathered all his weapons, his armor, and his potions.
But all he really needed, was one divine emotion.
He raged at the beast, and his skin grew hot,
his eyes grew feral, and he lost all thought.
And when the rage had ended, he once again became aware.
Now, lying at his feet, was the defeated umber bear."

The musical notes became visible with each strum of his instrument. In vivid colors of purple and red, they jumped from the lute and dispersed into the bodies of the three adventurers standing before him as Witt recited the second verse of his song.

He didn't have a lovely voice. He wasn't a bard capable of singing love songs to woo women, or captivating a crowd. No, he was a skald, a keeper of lore whose songs and poems had the power to send allies into a frenzied rage. The fact that he was a kobold, a reptilian race long believed to be the descendants of dragons, meant that his songs were not beautiful. Just like his voice, they were gruff. Oftentimes, they were angry. Every note he sang was rough and grating as it ripped through the air.

When the song finished, the adventurers turned and left without so much as a second glance at Witt.

The kobold took a seat on a nearby stump to wait until the next adventurer appeared. His post was along the path that led to the dungeon entrance. Tall, towering trees with skeletal limbs reached down from above. He had never been in the dungeon. He'd never been much of anywhere. For Witt, every day was the same. He woke, left his village of Murkwell, crossed the city of Skullheyden, and waited outside of the dungeon to sell his services to adventurers before they entered. At the end of the day, he'd go home, deposit his money into the village fund and wait for it all to start anew.

As he sat there, he saw Schekt, a fellow kobold and bartender of The Merry Minotaur Inn, passing by.

Witt waved to Schekt.

Schekt stopped and turned to Witt. "Greetings, adventurer! Welcome to The Merry Minotaur, would you like a room or a drink?"

Witt just shook his head. Every day, it was the same. Schekt walked by, said the same idiotic sentence, then carried on toward town. Schekt looked almost identical to Witt, with the same rust-colored scales, reptilian face, and ivory horns that protruded just behind his ears. Like all kobolds. Yet, he was the only kobold that behaved in this way. He must have been dropped on his head one too many times as a child. How he managed to run a bar, Witt had no idea.

The day passed slowly before the next group of adventurers appeared. Witt watched the swaying branches of the trees, not thinking about anything in particular.

He turned his head as a raucous party clamored their way over. A group of four dwarves laughed and bantered as they approached. A short stout dwarf carrying a warhammer smashed his weapon into the side of his party member. It clanked against the armor, dropping the dwarf's health by a chunk. The other two dwarves howled with laughter.

"Greetings, adventurers! How may I assist you today?" asked Witt.

"Shut up, kobold." The warhammer-wielding dwarf sneered, twisting his warhammer against his palm. He sported a thick red beard, braided intricately down his chest and adorned with silver clasps, and brown leather armor. "Give us your stupid buff."

The other three dwarves laughed even harder.

Witt took a step back, unsure why the adventurer was treating him with such hostility.

The bearded warrior stepped forward. "Buff, now," he growled.

Witt wasn't looking for trouble. In fact, he wanted to get the song over with so that these buffoons could be on their way. He extended his hand. "Five silver."

The group laughed as the warrior handed Witt the coins. An uneasy feeling passed through Witt that he couldn't quite explain. The scales on the back of his neck grew cold.

He strummed his lute, casting the party in a golden glow, then he began to sing. The party nodded their heads vigorously to his music, letting their thick locks whip through the air.

The entire experience had Witt on edge. Something was definitely off.

When Witt finished his song, a devious smirk spread across the warrior's face. A ring of purple energy swirled around each party member displaying that the buff had taken effect. The warrior laughed. It was icy, causing the patch of cold on Witt's neck to spread even farther.

"Thanks for the buff, kobold." The warrior smiled. "I've got a tip for you."

The other dwarves laughed.

Witt scrunched his nose; he'd never been given a tip before. Before he had time to understand what was happening, the warhammer connected with the side of his head. Witt's vision blurred, darkening around the edges. He tried to focus, but all he could think about was the ringing in his ears. Above the dull drone, laughter reigned.

A second blow brought Witt to his knees. He fought to stand, but it was no use. His world was darkness and laughter, then nothing at all.

CHAPTER TWO

Witt woke up in his bed. It was nothing spectacular, not like the fancy beds one might find at an inn in Skullheyden. This was nothing more than a collection of straw piled neatly in the burrow Witt shared with several other kobolds.

The kobold tunnels spread far and wide underneath the city, but the living quarters were in Murkwell to the North.

He stretched his arms overhead as he sat up and looked around, ready to start his day. Everyone else was gone. *I must have overslept.* Witt quickly threw on his clothing, grabbed his bag and his lute, and set off toward the dungeon entrance.

The sun was high in the sky as he raced from Murkwell to Skullheyden. Many of his fellow kobolds were already at work mining or farming. It was rare for a kobold to have a magical class, even rarer to have one like Witt's. Most kobolds who were blessed with magic were either assassins or rogues. But Witt loved his life, as strange as it may be. Helping heroes overcome dungeons was good work, and it kept the kingdom prospering. The money he made from each buff helped keep Murkwell prospering too.

Witt left the murky depths of Murkwell as fast as his

short reptilian legs would carry him. In the distance, the largest tower of Skullheyden castle stared down upon him. A massive stone skull with glowing pyres for eyes atop the tower comforted him in an ominous way.

He passed through the giant stone arches of the city entrance, catching a few stares from the guards, but they said nothing. The market bustled with heroes and townsfolk buying and selling. Witt scurried through the crowd, barely noticeable as he only came up to the waist of most of them.

Something bumped into Witt as he ran, knocking him off his feet.

"Watch where you're going!" a deep voice rumbled.

Witt looked up to see a stocky green orc snarling at him. A jagged scar ran diagonally from one corner of the orc's face to the other, and both of his tusks had been broken off, probably in battle.

"Kobolds." The orc shook his head. "Useless."

Witt ignored the remark. Kobolds had never gotten much respect, even though they took most of the jobs no one else wanted in the kingdom. Kobolds worked harder and longer than any other race, yet they were forced to live in burrows outside of the city.

It suited Witt just fine. He'd rather have the company of his fellow kobolds, even Schekt, over the hoity toity city dwellers. Evenings spent by the fire eating roasted meat and drinking kobold brew were some of his fondest memories.

After passing through the city, Witt followed the road to Cardamew Forest. After a mile, a haunting trail led into the depths of the forest where the famous Forgotten Quarters Dungeon awaited. A single adventurer stood at Witt's post looking around. The human woman wore all black, with nearly a dozen daggers strapped across her chest and legs.

When she spotted Witt, her blue eyes lit up. "There you

are! I was wondering if you would be coming back today. Those guys are a bunch of jerks."

Witt cocked an eyebrow, uncertain of what she was talking about.

"Greetings, adventurer! How may I assist you today?"

"I'd like a buff, please."

Witt played his lute and sung his song, and soon she was on her way.

He scratched his chin, his thick talons scraping over his tough scales. The sun was high overhead by this point. *How did I manage to sleep so late?* He'd always been an early riser as far back as he could remember. He shrugged and took a seat on the nearby stump. A moment later, the clank of plate armor announced a new arrival.

A knight in golden armor accompanied by two scantily clad females came to a stop in front of Witt. The kobold had never understood the practicality of the outfits many female adventurers wore. How this knight could cover everything but his eye holes, and yet these two women might lose their clothing in a stiff breeze was baffling.

Just one of the reasons that kobolds were far superior. One could hardly tell a female from a male based on clothing or appearance alone. Females might be smaller, but even then they didn't look that different from a young adult male.

The knight rested his massive shield on the ground and it sank into the earth several inches.

"Greetings, adventurers! How may I assist you today?" asked Witt.

The knight dropped to a knee. "We would like a buff before entering the dungeon."

"Five silver," replied Witt.

With payment exchanged, Witt strummed his lute and sang his song, casting them all in a glowing aura. Once finished, the knight stood, a purple ring of energy swirling around him and his companions. With a nod to Witt, they set off toward the dungeon.

"Out of my way!" someone shouted from the entrance to the dungeon.

Witt turned to see a group of three dwarves with dented armor, covered in blood and marching toward him. A red-bearded dwarf carrying a warhammer bumped into the knight without apology.

"Kobold! What kind of buff was that?" The dwarf's fingers flexed as he gripped his warhammer even tighter. "I thought you were supposed to make us invincible? One of our party died, and we barely made it out alive."

Witt looked on with confusion. He had never seen these three before in his life.

"I think you are mistaken, sir."

The dwarf shook his head. "Stupid, stupid kobold. You're going to pay for this. Give us the best buff you have and we'll go easy on you."

An icy cool crept across Witt's neck, putting him on edge. Why were these adventurers blaming him for their failure in the dungeon?

He extended his hand. "Five silver."

The dwarf laughed. "If you think I'm going to pay you after everything we just went through, you are sadly mistaken."

Witt raised his hands, hoping to calm the angry dwarf. "I'm sorry, sir, but rules are rules. The money for my services goes straight to the village."

One of the other dwarves put his hand on Red-beard's shoulder. "Come on, Stu, let's just get out of here."

Stu shrugged him off. "No. Jerry was almost level six and he lost all of that XP. This pathetic excuse for an NPC is going to pay. Again."

Again? What was this dwarf talking about? Surely, he has me mistaken for someone else.

"Come on, he's a kobold," the third dwarf chimed in. "They're worth practically zero XP. And this one is an NPC, not a monster. If someone catches you killing him, you'll have a bounty on your head. Is it really worth it?"

Stu glared at his party members. "Watch the path and make sure no one else comes this way."

With an exasperated sigh, the other two dwarves left, leaving Stu and Witt alone together.

The icy patch crept further down Witt's spine, and he suddenly had the urge to run. His thoughts drifted briefly to the daggers strapped to his side before he quickly pushed them away.

He was here to help the adventurers, not hurt them.

Something rustled in the nearby bushes, drawing the dwarf's attention. A kobold Witt recognized from a nearby burrow stepped onto the trail carrying a bundle of dead rabbits tied together with twine.

"Cerent? What are you doing here?" asked Witt. Considering the ire of the dwarf before him, this was not a great place for the kobold to be.

Cerent lifted the bundle of rabbits. "Heading to the market with my catch for the day."

Apparently, that was the end of the conversation for Cerent, because the kobold kept walking.

"Not so fast." Stu narrowed his eyes at Cerent, and then switched his focus to Witt. "I think it's time we teach you a lesson. My party will be back here tomorrow. Remember what happened here today and have a better buff waiting for us, or we can make your life very miserable."

Witt instinctively took a step back, bumping into the stump he had been sitting on.

Stu rushed forward and grabbed Cerent by the neck,

lifting him off the ground. The kobold squeaked in shock, letting the rabbits fall to the ground.

"Sir, please," pleaded Witt. "There must be some mistake."

Stu then grabbed Cerent by the feet, letting the kobold dangle upside down in his grip. With a spin, Stu swung the body of the kobold and smashed it into Witt. Witt tumbled to the ground, dazed.

He tried to crawl away, but Cerent's skull crashed into his own.

Cerent screamed in pain as Stu bludgeoned Witt again and again. Mad laughter echoed through the forest as Stu wielded the kobold like a whip. Witt's vision grew dark around the edges with each subsequent hit. Eventually, Cerent's screams faded. As Witt's vision shrunk to a pin-prick of light, the last thing he heard was Stu's icy voice.

"Don't forget."

CHAPTER THREE

Witt opened his eyes, surprised to find that it was evening. Even though he was underground, his internal clock always had accurate reading of the sun's positioning. *I must have been tired to sleep for so long.* It was the first time he could remember sleeping an entire day and missing his shift outside of the dungeon.

Outside of the burrow, many kobolds sat around a blazing fire. Others were scattered through the forest playing games and having fun. Nights in Murkwell were always filled with excitement. Once the drinks started flowing, anything was capable of happening.

"Greetings, adventurer! Welcome to The Merry Minotaur, would you like a room or a drink?" Schekt stumbled over, a clay cup in both hands, and handed one to Witt. No matter how many drinks he had, Schekt never forgot his lines.

"Thanks, Schekt." Witt took a sip of the brown liquid, and it filled his belly with warmth.

There was a loud bang and Witt looked up to see a blaze of light shooting across the forest. A smile crept across his face. They were using the kobold cannon.

Witt quickly chugged his drink and grabbed another. He'd need the liquid courage to take on the cannon.

Kobolds cheered as another bang filled the air and a streak of flame soared from one end of the burrow to the other. Oohs and ahhs swished through the forest. Witt walked up to the massive contraption that resembled a giant crossbow. It was a true depiction of kobold ingenuity and recklessness.

The kobold cannon had been one of the prized inventions of the kobold tinkerer Uggo. It was meant to launch kobolds over city walls so that they could wreak havoc during times of war. But it had been a while since the kobolds had gone to war, and now the cannon sat idle except for nights of revelry.

Witt watched as a kobold climbed a ladder onto the cannon. The cannon had a barrel in the center where the kobold would sit. One of Murkwell's tinkerers cranked a lever that pulled back the cables running from one bow iron to the other. Once it was cranked back far enough, the cables locked on a catch, and the weapon was ready to fire.

A third kobold climbed the ladder and handed a torch to the kobold about to be launched away.

The tinkerer then flipped a lever, launching the seated kobold into the air. The kobold screamed as he rocketed across the sky. The scream faded as he soared, and the light of the flame grew smaller before extinguishing entirely.

"Who's next?" asked Zirn, the tinkerer who had flipped the lever.

Zirn wore giant goggles with lenses that made him look like he had bug eyes.

"Me!" Witt raised his hand and rushed over.

"Step on up."

Witt climbed the ladder and took his position in the barrel. His heart raced at the thought of what was to come. He'd ridden the cannon a few times, and it was always exhilarating. For a few moments, he experienced what it was like to fly.

He took the torch in his hand, and waited as Zirn turned the crank. There was a loud click as the cable latched into place. A moment later, an enormous pressure surged into his back. His vision blurred as wind rushed against his eyes. The flames of the torch whipped like the sails of a ship at sea.

Witt felt weightless as he watched the kobolds below him scurrying about like ants. *This must be what it feels like to be a dragon.* It was said that kobolds descended from dragons, and that a little bit of that draconic fire still resided inside all kobolds. In that moment, Witt believed it.

A moment later, Witt's ascent slowed and he began to fall toward the earth. He braced for impact as he landed in the cool water of the landing area. Icy water chilled him to his core and extinguished the flame from his torch.

When Witt emerged from the pond, he couldn't stop grinning. He had the urge to do it again, but refrained. Best to let the others have some fun.

He returned to the fire and took a seat on a log. A wild boar roasted on a spit. Cerent, one of the kobolds from a neighboring burrow, rotated the boar so that it didn't burn.

"Howdy, Witt." Cerent flashed him a smile. "Care for some meat?"

"I'd love some. I haven't eaten all day." Witt still couldn't believe he had slept through an entire day.

Cerent pulled a knife from his belt and sliced off a hearty chunk of boar and handed it to Witt.

Witt's sharp teeth gnashed at the meat, ripping it apart. Juices trickled down his face and dripped onto his tunic.

Nearby, a fight broke out between two young kobolds. They tumbled on the ground, growling and squealing until some of the elders broke them up. It wasn't a party unless at least five fights broke out.

"Are you going to play us some music, Witt?" a voice asked.

Witt turned to see Kessy, a female kobold and one of his childhood friends, hovering next to him with glazed eyes. She had dark-black scales that faded to red around her snout, making her ivory horns stand out in the twilight. She took a sip of her drink.

"You know how your music livens up any get-together." She batted her eyes at him.

Witt couldn't argue with that. His songs had a profound effect on other kobolds, and he never turned down a request for a performance. He was the only skald in all of Murkwell after all.

"Give me a second to go grab my lute." Witt touched her on the arm and then disappeared back into the burrow.

He hurried through the tunnels to his burrow. Past the hatchery, where all of the unhatched kobold eggs sat comfortably around a warm fire, and past the traproom, where the tinkerers created traps for the king's dungeons. The entire underground was filled with rooms where kobold society thrived away from the city.

Most people never understood the pivotal role that kobolds played in society, but they were the silent majority, always working.

Witt found his lute propped against the dirt wall beside his bed. He grabbed it and rushed back to Kessy just in time to see another kobold blazing through the air overhead.

Taking a seat on a log, he strummed his lute and the forest grew quiet. Kobolds loved music, but they loved Witt's music above all. One by one, they gathered around the fire pit.

As the notes dispersed from the lute, lighting the forest like fireflies, dozens and dozens of kobolds emerged. Their bickering and raucousness stopped for the moment, and they stared in awe.

Witt placed his hand on the strings, and the music stopped. "This song goes out to kobolds one and all. You all know the words, so sing along."

A rapid stroke sent glowing musical notes erupting like a volcano to the cheers of the kobolds. Young kobolds reached out to grab the notes only to have them dissipate into their fingers.

Witt cleared his throat, and the song poured out of his mouth in a low growl.

"In ancient times, when lands were young,
and dragons spoke the only tongue,
they ruled the lands and skies above,
and hoarded all the things they loved.
But then came men and dwarves and elves,
who wanted treasures for themselves.
The dragons retreated into the highest mountains,
where only the bravest heroes found them.
It was in this time kobolds were born,
to protect the dragons and their hoard.
They fought with axes, spears, and knives,
and made elaborate traps to hide.
They caught the heroes unaware..."

As Witt continued to sing, his words ripping at the very fabric of time and space, a change came over the kobolds listening. They joined him in song and their eyes, glazed from countless drinks of kobold brew, began to glow red. Their scales grew hot, and a frenzy snaked among them.

As a skald, Witt's songs had the power to enrage his people far beyond the buffs he could offer other races. In times of war, skalds were considered an integral part of kobold battle strategy, making their warriors stronger and tougher through the power of music.

Witt jumped into the second verse and the tempo increased as he sang of the kobolds' battles against great heroes, and eventual formation of their own society. By the time he finished, those surrounding him were foaming at the mouth.

"Attack the troll!" Zirn raised his fist into the air.

Hisses and growls answered his call as snarling kobolds rushed into the depths of the forest. The forest troll was a constant blight on Murkwell, and many kobolds had wandered into its lands to never return. Witt followed along with interest to see what might become of the raging kobolds.

When enough kobolds were affected by his music, he'd seen them battle ogres and direwolves, but never a troll. This would be most interesting.

Zirn led the charge. Next to him, Tigra directed a group of well-trained direweasels. Witt continued to play and sing, keeping the frenzy going as they marched through the forest.

They came into a clearing of broken trees. The entire area had been flattened by the troll who lived here. Normally, kobolds avoided this area of the forest, but this wasn't a normal night. This was a night for the kobolds to prove to themselves that they deserved respect.

A slumbering troll lay in the center of the clearing, a half-eaten boar still gripped in its hand. The troll was a dull grey, with a bulbous nose and boils covering its shoulders and arms. Snot bubbles rose and fell as it snored thunderously. Its large, fat belly inflated with each breath. A dozen kobolds crawled on its body without waking it.

The kobolds swarmed the monster before it had a chance to wake. Witt watched in respectful horror as several direweasels burrowed inside of the troll's massive nostrils and attacked.

The troll sat up in alarm, grabbing its nose and stomping

kobolds left and right in a blind rage. The deaths didn't bother the kobolds, for they believed that every death was a rebirth, and their essence would hatch again in a continuous cycle.

Witt continued to strum and sing, invigorating the kobolds with righteous fury. A blast of fire soared over Witt's shoulder and he turned to see Hux, the only kobold mage in Murkwell, with fiery red eyes as he cast fire from his staff.

The fireball collided with the troll in an explosion, bursting boils to the sound of sizzling flesh. For every kobold that was stomped or tossed aside, another took its place. They bit and they stabbed, swarming like ants on the overwhelmed troll.

Kessy climbed over her brothers and planted two daggers in the eyes of the troll. It screamed in pain, blindly grabbing her and thrusting her into a nearby tree. Her body crumpled to the ground at the impact.

For a moment, his heart sank at the loss of his friend, but he knew she would be reborn in the hatchery. She might not be the Kessy he knew, but no kobold was ever truly gone.

With the troll blinded, the kobolds quickly gained the upper hand. A final fireball to the face was all it took to send the monster into an eternal slumber.

CHAPTER FOUR

Witt wiped the sleep from his eyes, ready to start the day. He grabbed his pack and his lute and set off for the Forgotten Quarters dungeon.

On his way, he passed Kessy by the hatchery.

"Good luck out there today, Witt." She winked at him before heading off to her own post in the nearby mountain where she mined for metals and precious jewels.

Mining was by far the most common job for kobolds, followed by farming and hunting. Then there were those who worked in the city, like Schekt. Kobolds with classes like Witt's or Hux's, the mage, were extremely uncommon.

The sun was only beginning to rise as Witt made his way across Skullheyden square. The vendors in the market were setting up their tables for the day, and the shop-keepers scurried in their shops making sure everything was in order.

Soon, the heroes would be arriving to make their purchases for the day and setting out on their next adventure.

A line of heroes waited for Witt when he arrived at his post outside of the dungeon. He sang his song, buffing a party of elves, and then a mixed party consisting of an orc, a dwarf, and a human.

The day had just started and Witt had already made ten silver for the village. *This is looking like a great day already.*

By noon, he had buffed nearly twenty parties before they entered the dungeon. During a brief respite, he sat on a tree stump and ate the lunch he had packed for the day. He ripped into a sliver of boar jerky and enjoyed the peppery goodness.

"There he is," a voice called from down the path. "Look at him eating, like he doesn't have a care in the world."

Witt turned to see a party of four dwarves making their way toward him. He put away his food and grabbed his lute, ready to buff them with a song.

The party consisted of a warrior with a braided red beard holding a warhammer, a brown-bearded mage wearing a blue robe and carrying a gnarled staff tipped with a sapphire, a grey-bearded paladin in white armor with a billowing cloak and carrying a massive shield engraved with a lightning emblem, and a black-bearded rogue wearing black leather armor and wielding a crossbow.

"Greetings, adventurers! How may I assist you today?" Witt smiled.

"Greetings, adventurers! How may I assist you today?" The red-bearded warrior mocked him. "No matter what we do to you, you're never going to remember." He tilted his head back and laughed.

Witt scrunched his eyes, unsure of what the dwarf was talking about.

The others joined in, but the paladin wore an uncertain expression. "Why don't you just give him a break for once, Stu?"

"Come on, dude, lighten up. He's a kobold. They were practically invented for our entertainment. They're like goblins, only dumber."

"You're like a goblin, but dumber." The rogue smirked. "And you're obsessed. What did this kobold ever do to you?"

Witt took a step back. It was like they were having a conversation about him, but he'd never seen these four in his life. It was all a bit unsettling.

"I'm sorry, sirs, but you must have me mistaken. I know we all look alike." He tried to lighten the mood with a joke. "Would you like a buff so that you can be on your way?"

The warrior dwarf, Stu, narrowed his eyes. "I'll tell you when we're ready for your stupid buff." He looked to his party members.

Witt stood in stunned silence. There was no need for this dwarf to be so rude to him. He contemplated leaving, but then that would mean less money for the village. No, he would deal with the awkwardness of the situation and then soon they would be gone.

Witt nodded. "Whenever you are ready, sir."

Stu smiled. "That's more like it. Maybe I'm getting through to you after all. Go ahead with the buff. We want the best one you've got."

Seething on the inside, Witt forced a smile as he stroked his lute. Little did the dwarves know that Witt was only capable of two buffs. The one he used on heroes to increase their Strength and Constitution, and the one he used on the kobolds to send them into a frenzy. So whatever these dwarves thought they might get from him in addition to the normal buff, they would be sorely disappointed.

"Five silver." He held out his hand.

After the dwarf paid him, Witt softly sang.

"It was a day, a normal day, when Scrabolt became aware,
that deep within the mountain's caves, there lived a mighty bear.
The bear was strong and hardy, but Scrabolt was as well..."

The notes from his lute dispersed with each strum, visibly

shooting from the strings and drifting through the air before diffusing into the dwarves' bodies.

Witt watched the heroes, in particular the way the warrior stared at him with a mixture of amusement and annoyance, as he sang the words branded into his memory without thinking.

He finished the song, leaving the party swirling in a purple aura, and waited for them to leave.

Three of the dwarves turned to go, but Stu continued to stare at Witt.

An icy patch formed on the back of his neck. The longer Stu stared, the more it spread.

"Come on, Stu. Let's go." The mage grabbed Stu by the arm. "You've tortured him enough."

Stu pulled away. "Just one more." He smirked. "For old time's sake."

The paladin rolled his eyes. "Sorry, little dude."

Stu lifted his warhammer and gave it a spin.

Witt couldn't explain why, but he had the sudden urge to run. He gave into his instincts and took off toward the city. Before he had even made it two steps, something smashed into his back, knocking him to the ground.

He rolled over just in time to see Stu's warhammer flying through the air and returning to his hand.

Don't forget.

The words flashed across Witt's mind. He'd heard them somewhere before.

Stu stalked toward Witt with his warhammer tossed over his shoulder. The purple aura Witt had buffed the dwarf with flared with energy.

Don't forget.

Stu appeared in Witt's mind. He held Cerent, using the kobold's body as a weapon, beating Witt over and over until both kobolds were dead.

Witt didn't move, still inside his own mind, as the warhammer hit him across the face. His vision went white and images flooded his mind. It was like a dam had broken, filling him with memories long lost.

He screamed at the brutality that flashed before him, and for a moment, Stu stood frozen.

Witt was lost to the world as he relived every death he had ever experienced at the hands of the so-called heroes.

A minotaur gripped him around the throat before dropping him hundreds of feet into the infamous pit on the edge of Skullheyden.

A barbarian had thought it funny to see how far he could toss the kobold. Witt had landed with enough force to crack his skull like a melon.

He had been used as a weapon by a paladin in the same manner as Cerent until his eyes burst from his skull.

"What's he doing?" someone asked, but Witt was still blinded.

He relived being eaten by a druid who had transformed into a bear. It had ripped his arm clean off.

A tamer kidnapped him and took him into the forest to feed to a large spider. The clicking of the pincers echoed in his mind as his body sat trapped in a cocoon of silk.

A fighter cut off his limbs one by one to test the sharpness of his blades.

A ranger shot him with arrows as target practice.

A mage burned him alive.

One by one, the memories came flooding back and Witt relived every one. When the visions stopped, he opened his eyes.

Stu took a step back. "What in the hell just happened?"

Cold rage spread through Witt like morning frost. "I remember."

Witt snarled. Cold hatred pulsed in his veins. He

launched himself at the dwarf without thinking, drawing his daggers and aiming for the neck. He would kill this dwarf that had caused him so much pain.

Stu raised his warhammer, using it as a shield to block the attack. He parried Witt aside, but Witt wasn't done. He wanted to make him pay. He wanted to make everyone pay.

He charged again, but this time Stu was ready. His warhammer glowed red as it connected with Witt's shoulder. Bones cracked and the small kobold crumpled to the ground.

The last thing he saw was the head of the warhammer before everything went black.

CHAPTER FIVE

Witt woke to the sound of his own screams.

"They killed me!" he shouted, but the burrow was empty. His words echoed off the walls, every bit as hollow as Witt felt.

His internal clock told him that it was early afternoon, and everyone was at their posts for the day.

Witt pulled his knees to his chest, his thoughts consumed by what had just happened. For years, he had been waking up every day with no memory of the awful things he had endured. It was like those horrible memories had been wiped day in and day out. For the first time in his life, he realized that waking up in the afternoon with no one around was not oversleeping, it was respawning.

He was cold all over. Icy rage emanated from his core.

For so long, he had believed that he was doing good work, that he was helping the noble heroes on their pursuits of greatness and bravery. But now he knew the truth, they weren't heroes. They were monsters.

Witt shook with anger. He'd spent years trying to be the helpful kobold, and this was how he had been repaid? It wasn't right. But he could make it right. He'd give them what he'd received.

And worse.

He wanted revenge, but how? Clearly, he wasn't strong enough to take on the heroes. The many times he had died proved that.

He raked his nails over his scales. There had to be something he could do. He would go talk to Hux. If he could convince the mage to join him, then maybe they could give the heroes a dose of their own medicine.

Witt grabbed his items and rushed down the tunnel. He froze in his tracks when he noticed something flashing in the corner of his vision. A tiny image of a kobold pulsed before him. He tried to reach out and touch it, but whatever he was seeing, it was like it was in his mind, not reality.

As he focused on the flashing image, it grew larger. With an audible click, the image of a grey kobold expanded into a sheet of parchment.

Name: *Witt*
  Race: *Kobold*
  Class: *Skald (Barbarian/Bard hybrid)*
  Level: *4*

STRENGTH: *10*
  DEXTERITY: *14*
  CONSTITUTION: *12*
  INTELLIGENCE: *8*
  WISDOM: *10*
  CHARISMA: *15*

He stared at the display before him, wondering briefly if he was going insane. Deep inside, he knew it wasn't true. He had stumbled upon something that he had been missing his entire life. It was as if a veil had been lifted and for the first time, he was seeing the world as it truly was. He couldn't explain it, but he knew that the heroes had access to this kind of information.

The real question was what would he do with this knowledge?

He examined the sheet of parchment floating in his vision further. There was a section that listed his equipment and his proficiency with daggers and his lute. Below that, his clothing was itemized. At the very bottom, he found his skills and abilities.

Skills: Darkvision, Perception, Languages (Common, Draconic), Pack Stratagem, Music, Lore.

Beneath that was a list of abilities.

Abilities (available): As a skald, you gain one ability per level, alternating between bard and barbarian abilities.

Skaldic songs: Only one song may buff a party at a given time. Affected allies must be able to hear the skald for the song to have any effect. Deaf creatures, as well as undead, elementals, and constructs are not affected by songs.

---

1. **Inspired Frenzy (bard):** Increases Strength and Constitution of kobolds while sending them into a rage. The caster may also choose to accept the effects.

A raging song can be disrupted, and it ends immediately if the skald is killed, paralyzed, stunned, silenced, or incapacitated.

2. **Strong Hand (barbarian):** Hold a two-handed weapon in one hand.

3. **Ballad of the Bold (bard):** Increases Strength and Constitution of non-kobold allies.

4. **Cleave (barbarian):** Attacks deal splash damage in an arc.

Seeing his abilities listed out like this was an odd feeling. Knowing that he was level four out of gods only knew how many levels was a bit shocking. His mind wandered to the heroes who had killed him, and he wondered what level they might be.

Whatever level they are, I need to be stronger.

Witt took a deep breath and continued down the tunnel until he came to the hatchery. Something was different. A bar with words floated above each egg.

Kobold Egg
   HP:10/10

He quickly found that by focusing on the eggs, he could make their health bars disappear and reappear at will. He stared at the dozens of floating bars, each one so small, even compared to his own. The future of his people rested in these tiny eggs. He stared at them, mesmerized that the entire life force of each egg was contained in something so abstract. Something only he could see.

How many of them would grow up just to be tortured in the same ways Witt had been? How many of his fellow kobolds had already been killed for amusement?

A fresh wave of anger pulsed inside his chest. With a snarl on his face, Witt set off to find Hux.

He passed several kobolds along the way to Corvin Mountain. Most of the kobolds he passed were low-level farmers or miners with barely one hundred health points. Had they been killed by some hero to end up back in Murkwell this early in the day, or was he just being paranoid?

Anger powered every step as Witt marched toward the mountain. He'd never had a quick temper. By all accounts, Witt was friendly and charming, but as his brow furrowed and the patch of cool calming ice rested on his shoulders, he found that it comforted him.

He refused to be a victim any longer.

CHAPTER SIX

Witt shifted through bouts of anger and amazement as he followed a well-traveled dirt road that led from Skullheyden to Corvin Mountain. He could turn on his ability to analyze living beings and items at will. When the hovering bars over a crowded street became too distracting, he turned them off to focus on his plan.

His world had forever changed, and he would do his best to make sure no other kobolds suffered at the hands of the heroes. To get started, he would need to talk to the strongest kobold he knew, Hux.

Hux was the most powerful kobold in Murkwell, and the only mage. Every day, he traveled up to Corvin Mountain, where he would defend the pass from giant wolf spiders as they attempted to take over the road. Failure not only meant that they could attack the city, but they would devour the unattended eggs in the hatchery if they made it to Murkwell.

If anyone would know what to do, it would be Hux.

Something bumped into Witt, drawing him from his thoughts and knocking him to the ground. As a kobold, he was constantly in danger of being trampled by larger beings.

"Easy there, little one." A massive hand extended from the blue minotaur hovering over Witt. "You don't want to get stepped on."

Fear pulsed through Witt as he pulled his dagger from his belt and pointed it at the minotaur, causing the towering hero to recoil. "Stay back," he snarled, shoving the blade upward. There was no way he was letting another hero put their hands on him.

The minotaur raised his hands and took a step back. "Easy, now. I was just trying to help."

"I don't need your help," Witt spat as he crawled to his feet, never lowering his weapon.

A second hero, a female human wearing a flowing gown, grabbed the minotaur by the arm. "What's gotten into him? Isn't this the same kobold that buffs us outside of the dungeon on the other side of the city?"

The minotaur rolled his eyes. "Suzie, that's racist. They don't all look the same. The dungeon kobold has always been nice to us. I don't know what's gotten into this one, but let's just leave him be."

The duo turned and left, and Witt finally released the breath he had been holding. He wouldn't be fooled by their false niceties. His heart thundered in his chest. *That was a close one.*

For the rest of his journey, Witt kept his focus on those around him, steering clear of the many heroes that were journeying into the mountain. Corvin Mountain was home to several dungeons and quests, so the roads leading into the mountain were always packed.

Witt silently seethed as he watched the heroes walking around without a care in the world. One of them carried the carcass of a large wolf over his shoulder as he headed back toward the city. How many of them had to worry about being killed just for existing?

A group of three orcs hurried past, and Witt caught the tail-end of their conversation.

"We're supposed to help this kobold mage defend the pass. There's a loot drop that should help me with my next potion, but we need to hurry before he leaves his post for the day."

Witt increased his pace, following the three orcs. After a while, they came upon a wooden sign that pointed to Mach-muller Pass. The three orcs left the main road, venturing onto a dirt trail that led deeper into the mountain.

Witt let them go ahead before continuing on their trail, careful not to be seen.

The green-skinned orcs were lumbering creatures as they ventured down the narrow path. With broad shoulders and thick thighs, they crunched branches with reckless abandon, uncaring of who or what might notice them.

Witt, on the other hand, moved almost silently. He walked on the tips of his toes, carefully avoiding branches and leaves. Centuries of their ancestors sneaking around to avoid death had made the kobolds experts at becoming unnoticed. This inevitably led to the occasional rotten apple that would venture down the path of becoming a thief or rogue.

An explosion from further up the path caused the orcs to take off running. Witt followed in close pursuit.

As he crested the hill, Witt found Hux with his staff extended, a wall of flame blocking the path in front of him. The three orcs came to a stop next to the mage.

Hux turned to the orcs. "Valiant heroes, the pass is under siege by a pack of wolf spiders. I cannot hold them alone. Help me defeat the foul monsters and you shall find yourself greatly rewarded."

Valiant heroes. Witt snorted in indignation. They would probably stab Hux in the back as soon as the quest was over.

"We accept." The tallest of the three orcs pulled the axe

strapped to his back and held it at the ready.

The other two took a fighting stance slightly behind him. Although they were dressed in similar garb, it was clear that each hero had a different role. The orc to the right held a massive bone in the same manner as Hux's staff. The one to the left wielded a pair of twin daggers, though they would have been swords in Witt's hands.

The flames of Hux's wall began to fade, revealing the monstrous creatures on the other side.

Spiders larger than Witt clicked their pincers together, and one of the orcs took a step back. Hair vibrated on the spiders' furry legs, sharp talons dug into the earth, and a collection of milky eyes gazed back at them.

The fire wall faded and the spiders charged down the mountain pass. Hux hurled a fireball from his staff, hitting the frontrunner in the face. The blast singed the fur, revealing a grotesque form underneath.

The axe-wielding orc rushed in, swinging his weapon with enough force to slice through two legs. The beast toppled to one side, black ichor spurting from its shortened appendages.

While the orc hacked away, several spiders leapt over their fallen comrade, launching themselves at the other two orcs.

The orc on the right raised his bone scepter and the tip glowed purple. A loud crack formed in the mountainside and stone broke away, falling and crushing one of the wolf spiders. Its legs curled up as its abdomen exploded in a spray of black jelly.

The dagger-wielding orc suddenly moved with much more finesse than he had on the journey here. Almost like a switch had been flipped. He dodged the claw-tipped legs of the wolf spiders, spinning and slashing, painting the ground with streaks of black all the while Hux pummeled the spiders with fireballs.

Several spiders now lay dead, but more appeared on the pass.

The icy patch on Witt's neck grew as he watched his kinsman helping the heroes to grow stronger. Every spider they killed put them one step closer to hurting his people.

They should all die. A streak of cold shot down his spine.

If an opportunity presented itself, then Witt would make sure they didn't complete the quest.

The orc mage seemed to have an affinity for earth magic. He continuously toppled rocks from the mountainside and drew stalagmites from the earth to pierce the spiders from beneath.

Witt suddenly remembered his ability to see their stats and focused on the heroes. His suspicion of the mage was confirmed. He could also see that the axe-wielder was a barbarian, and the one with the daggers was a rogue.

Surprisingly, though, they were only level six. Hux, on the other hand, was level eight. If he could win Hux to his cause, then they could likely take them on.

Before he knew it, Hux and the orcs had defeated seven of the monstrous spiders. At level six, they had been fairly evenly matched. The barbarian and rogue orcs had taken quite the beating and sat at fifty percent health as the final wolf spider, a level seven boss, stalked toward them.

This spider was much larger and covered in gray-tipped fur. A toxic-looking substance coated the pincers that clicked in its grotesque mouth.

The orc mage summoned a rock slide, but the boulders bounced off the boss's hardened carapace barely doing any damage.

The barbarian cursed. "This is going to be tough."

A violent scream tore through the mountainside as the orc mage was hit with a glob of acidic spit. His health bar rapidly dropped as the acid burned his green skin.

Excitement flared through Witt and his hands shook with anticipation. This was his opportunity. If he waited for the perfect moment to strike, he could take out one of the heroes while they fought the boss spider.

The rogue and barbarian split apart and charged in. The milky eyes of the spider divided to both sides as the orcs tried to split its attention. While the orcs rushed in, Hux cast a fireball that exploded on the spider's abdomen, singeing more hair and revealing a shimmering carapace much tougher than the other spiders'.

Witt slowly crept toward them, a dagger in both hands.

A massive leg pinned the rogue to the ground with a thud, sending his daggers soaring through the air. One of them clanked off the mountain and the other stabbed point-down a foot in front of Witt.

He put one of his daggers away and pulled the weapon from the earth. Using his Strong Hand ability, he was able to wield what would normally be a two-handed weapon with one arm.

Chaos reigned around him as the barbarian and the two mages fought to save the rogue's life. The claw-tipped leg had drawn blood, and pressed deeper into the rogue's chest with each passing second.

Serves him right. A dark laugh settled inside of Witt.

He was feet away from the orc mage when the barbarian shouted.

"We're almost there! Hit it with everything we've got!"

A flare of energy pulsed through the barbarian. Steam radiated from his skin and his muscles bulged with renewed vigor. His swings grew more intense as rage flooded his veins.

The orc mage raised his bone scepter into the air and for a moment, he stood still. The tip of the scepter flashed bright blue and a chasm ripped through the pass. The hind legs of the spider fell in, loosening its grip on the rogue.

Hux summoned a wall of flame in the new-formed pit and the spider's health trickled down more and more as the arachnid struggled to climb free.

The barbarian leapt into the flaming pit after the monster. His increased regeneration negated the flames that engulfed the spider below him.

While the battle raged on, Witt seized his opportunity. He raised the stolen sword overhead, ready to strike the unsuspecting mage.

As he brought the blade down, a final death scream escaped the spider, and the mage hurried forward, leaving Witt swiping at air.

Hux turned as the sword clattered against the ground. "Witt? What are you doing here?"

The three orcs turned to face him.

"I, uh." Witt searched for an explanation. Now that the battle was over, he had squandered his opportunity. He lifted the sword. "I found this down the path."

He forced a smile and walked over to the orc, handing him the weapon. The rogue ignored Witt, equipping his weapon and downing a health potion before returning to Hux.

The kobold mage greeted the orcs with a smile. "Thank you for your service in defending the kingdom from dangerous threats. You'll find your rewards among the corpses."

The orcs rifled through the bodies, collecting hairy spider legs and a mana crystal from the boss. They took their rewards and disappeared back down the path, talking amongst themselves and not sparing a second glance at Witt or Hux.

"What are you doing all the way out here?" Hux stood next to Witt. "You're a long way from the dungeon."

A scowl crossed Witt's face. "We need to talk."

CHAPTER SEVEN

Hux's black eyes pierced into Witt. "I don't believe it." He shook his head before walking over to the edge of the path that provided a sweeping view of the valley below. There was a steep drop from where they stood, several hundred feet of mountainside with exposed boulders and remnants from trees that once grew there before a rockslide had toppled them into the valley. "When kobolds die, we are reborn in the hatchery. This is the way it has always been. If what you say is true, then what would be the point of all those eggs?"

Witt sighed. "I don't know. The eggs are real. I've seen the life that resides in them, but I know what I have experienced. What I have seen. I get the feeling that the heroes aren't here to help right the world. This is a game to them. One where we pay the price."

Hux gazed out into the wilderness, lost in thought, when Witt had an idea.

"I can prove it to you." Witt's eyes flared with intensity and mischief.

Hux squinted one of his eyes. "How do you plan to do that?"

"Kill me." He stood up straight. "Kill me, and then return to the burrow. You'll find me there waking up in my own bed."

Hux laughed. When he realized Witt was serious, the mage leaned in, taking a long sniff. "Isn't it a bit early to be drinking kobold brew? What you're talking about is insane."

Witt didn't have time to wait for Hux to come around. The mage was powerful, but he had a high regard for kobold life. He wouldn't kill the only skald in Murkwell to test out a theory. Up until today, neither would Witt. But a lot had changed since morning. If he had any chance of winning Hux to his cause, then he would have to offer irrefutable evidence that he could respawn.

He needed to prove to the mage once and for all that he was telling the truth. Witt stepped to the edge of the path, kicking a rock and watching it tumble down the mountainside.

He had to act fast before Hux had a chance to try and stop him. Witt took a deep breath and gathered his resolve.

"Meet me at the burrow." He winked at the mage and flung himself from the mountain.

Hux stared at him in wild wonder, jaw hanging open, as Witt descended toward pain and disfigurement.

For a brief moment, Witt felt weightless. It was like he was in the kobold cannon all over again, wind whipping against his eyes, the fire of the dragon burning within him.

And then gravity took hold with a vengeance. His shoulder shattered as he made impact with a boulder, scales splitting to reveal dark-red flesh underneath. Blackness coated the edges of his vision as he plunged down the mountain, rocks and tree stumps assaulting his body. Stars flashed before him as his entire body crunched and ripped apart.

He tumbled head over tail before striking another boulder that broke his leg, twisting it at an odd angle. His entire world was pain and dizziness. Witt rocketed high into the air again. He roared in agony and his screams echoed off the mountains.

Broken and defeated, Witt welcomed the final impact as everything turned black.

CHAPTER EIGHT

Witt grabbed his shoulder, but there was no pain. Still, the memories of his fall echoed in his mind. Would it be enough to convince Hux? He hoped so.

He sat up in the empty burrow and pulled his legs to his chin. It would be a while before Hux showed up. In the meantime, Witt would spend some time in Murkwell. He had never really explored the daily life of his fellow kobolds. His days had been spent in service of his community, helping heroes in exchange for gold. But as far as he was concerned, his time buffing heroes for the Forgotten Quarters Dungeon was over.

The time had come to forge a new path. He would make the heroes regret the day they had decided to toy with him.

Witt made his way down the tunnel, past the traproom and once again stopping in front of the hatchery. Hux did have a point. If all kobolds respawned, then what was the purpose for all of these eggs? He took a long glance at the eggs before shrugging and setting off for aboveground. There would be time for existential thought once he had convinced Hux to join his cause.

A loud crash stopped Witt in his tracks, followed by a mad cackle that echoed down the tunnel.

Carefully, Witt snuck back down the tunnel, coming to a stop outside of the traproom. The traproom was where the tinkerers tested out new inventions. He hadn't noticed anyone inside after respawning, but peeking around the corner he found Zirn chuckling to himself as he swept up the debris of a crushed bloodmelon.

Several more bloodmelons lay in a pile against the wall. The melons had a pasty white exterior and a dark-red center. Their bitter taste made them practically inedible to most races. Minotaurs had a strange obsession with them, though.

In Murkwell, they were used widely to test the effectiveness of kobold traps since their innards did a good job of showcasing how the trap would affect a living creature. Plus, they were much easier to come by than living subjects. At least willing ones.

The traps they created protected the village, but more importantly, the king of Skullheyden paid top coin for new ways to guard the secret entrances into his kingdom.

Zirn stabbed his claw into a bit of the fleshy melon before tossing it into the fire pit against the back wall. There was a flash and a sizzle as the flames devoured the debris and smoke funneled up a small tunnel to the surface.

Witt stepped into the room. "Working on a new trap?"

Zirn glanced up, his goggles magnifying his dark-black eyes. They glittered with excitement. "Wait until you see this!"

The kobold tinkerer continued to talk as he worked his way around the room. "What we have here is a trap tile." He pointed to the floor, where a stone tile rested on a set of springs. "It will be placed in the center of one of the old tunnels beneath the castle. Ohze will paint it up nicely so that it doesn't look out of place." Zirn crouched and pointed to the center of the springs, where a button attached to a wire that ran up the wall of the tunnel. The wire attached to an oddly shaped contraption mounted near the ceiling above both sides of the tile. "When enough weight steps on the tile, it will trigger this button."

Above the tile, a tall piece of wood supported a bloodmelon at about the same height as a human head. Zirn pressed hard on the tile and then immediately backed out of the way. There was a quick whir as the button activated, tightening the wire and activating the trap. Two sharp projectiles launched from the ceiling, colliding with the melon and exploding the fruit from the inside out.

Witt instinctively took a step back as shrapnel and melon gore rained down around him. Zirn laughed even more maniacally as he swept up the carnage.

"What was that?" asked Witt.

Zirn smirked. "Glass projectiles." He picked up a box off a nearby table and it rattled as he tilted it for Witt to see. "Even better than wood or metal, because they break off into shards inside of whatever they hit."

Inside were dozens of glass spears the size of Witt's forearm. The tips were incredibly pointy. No wonder they had impaled the melon so easily.

Zirn picked one out of the box and tapped his fingertip against the pointed end of the spear. "They're sharp enough to impale bone, but when they hit one another—" He raised his brow suggestively. "—Well, you saw."

An idea popped into his mind, igniting the patch of ice that had become a fixture on the back of his neck. *What if I put one of these outside of the dungeon?* His heart raced at the thought of glass exploding inside of Stu's skull. How satisfying that would be.

"What other traps do you have?" Witt salivated for more

ways to give back some of the pain he had endured so many times.

Zirn's eyes lit up again. It must not be often that he had the chance to talk about his inventions. He ushered Witt over to a large shelving unit carved into the far wall.

"What don't we have? The top row is projectiles. Arrows, poisoned darts, flesh-eating worms." He pointed to two jars on the shelf below. "If you mix these two powders together, you get a nasty explosion. We've got caltrops, spikes, trip wires. But these are all just accessories. The key to any successful trap is in the execution. We test out the design here and then we build it custom to each location so that it is practically undetectable."

Witt activated his analyze skill on the contents on the shelf.

Item: Poisoned Dart. *Deals 1% poison damage per second.*

Item: Boom Powder. *This dangerous combustible creates intense heat when its core ingredients are combined. Inflicts burn damage.*

Creature: Flesh-eating Worm. *Invertebrates capable of devouring living flesh. Though not particularly fast, once burrowed beneath the skin, they can eat through both flesh and bone.*

A grin spread across Witt's face. He could definitely do some serious damage with these items.

"If I needed a trap made, do you think you could help me out?" asked Witt.

Zirn furrowed his brow. "I don't see why not, but what could a skald possibly be doing to have need of a trap?"

Witt smirked. "When I find out, I'll let you know."

He left Zirn to his inventions and pondered ideas for revenge as he strolled down the tunnel. The savory smell of stew caused his belly to rumble and Witt realized just how hungry he was. He was famished. Death really had a way of zapping his energy.

He followed his snout until he came to Knoma's Stewery, where a continuous cauldron of stew was always boiling. It had been rumored that the same stew had been boiling since the kobolds first settled in Murkwell. Witt wasn't sure how much truth there was to it, but he'd never found a stew so delicious anywhere outside of Murkwell.

Knoma leaned over the butcher's block chopping pieces of rabbit and tossing them into the cauldron. She nodded at Witt as he entered.

Knoma was one of the older Kobolds. So old that her scales had begun to fade around her snout and her talons had turned gray. A tattered apron hung from her neck, stained from years of use. She wasn't one for idle chit chat, but she made one hell of a stew.

Witt grabbed a clay bowl and scooped himself a healthy helping. The savory broth went down easy, and the hint of spice left his throat tingling with each gulp. He slurped every last drop and then ate the meat residing in the bottom of the bowl. With a full belly, Witt offered his thanks and left.

Aboveground, Murkwell was mostly empty. A few hunters traveled here and there and a handful of kobolds sat on the bank of the creek fishing. Most kobolds were either mining in Corvin Mountain, farming at a nearby village, or working menial jobs in Skullheyden.

Murkwell wasn't a hot destination for heroes. There were trolls, ogres, and other creatures just outside of its boundaries, but there was very little for them to do in the village itself. Not to mention that the burrows underground were too small for most heroes to maneuver through comfortably.

Witt took some small solace in the fact that even though his people suffered at the hands of the heroes, their village had remained largely untouched.

A patter of feet caught Witt's attention and he turned to see Tigra training her direweasels. She wore a fur shawl and leather bracers on both arms. The furry creatures raced back and forth on an obstacle course among the trees, jumping through hoops, climbing ropes, and honing their agility and teamwork. Three direweasels stood one on top of the other, grabbing a rock that was attached to a rope hanging from a tall limb.

"What are you doing out here?" Witt accepted the rock that the direweasel had brought him.

Tigra took her eyes off of her pets and turned to Witt. "Morning is for adventure, afternoon is for training. You never can be too prep—"

"You son of a banshee!" Hux stormed in their direction, his face contorted in anger. He threw his staff to the ground and grabbed Witt by the tunic, lifting him off the ground. "Explain yourself! I saw you die."

Witt had never seen Hux so angry, but he didn't fight back. This was part of the process. One didn't simply discover that their entire existence was a fabrication and pretend like everything was fine.

As his brains rattled in his skull, Witt watched as realization dawned on Hux. His features twisted from anger to sadness, and then finally, an uncomfortable acceptance. Hux released Witt and he fell to the ground.

Witt dusted himself off, and looked Hux square in the eye. "Are you done? Because I need your help with a little vengeance."

CHAPTER NINE

"And they did it for no other reason than because they could?" Hux's stiff posture and intense gaze was new to Witt. "How many times has this happened to me? To all of us?" He slammed the butt of his staff against the ground. "They will pay dearly for this."

Witt smiled. It felt good to have the most powerful kobold in Murkwell on his side. Together, they could finally show these heroes that kobolds were more than just entertainment.

They passed through Skullheyden and soon found themselves at Witt's normal location on the path to the Forgotten Quarters Dungeon. A small crowd had formed, waiting for a chance to be buffed.

When Witt and Hux walked past the group without comment, an elven archer called out. "Hey, aren't you going to buff us?"

Witt flashed them a rude gesture without glancing over his shoulder. "Get your own buffs."

He held his head high, smirking as he imagined the looks on their faces.

The entrance to the Forgotten Quarters Dungeon was forgettable by most accounts. An unobtrusive archway made from stone that led underground. A single lantern hung outside the door above a wooden sign detailing the dungeon's name.

Witt caught a glimpse of a piece of glittering platemail before it disappeared into the depths below. His neck grew cold as the hero vanished out of sight. The dwarves were likely long gone, but it didn't matter. All heroes were the same. They only cared about themselves. He'd died at the hands of enough of them to know that Stu and the other dwarves weren't outliers.

They were the norm.

Witt turned to Hux. "Ready?"

Hux's normally black eyes burned red. "Ready."

With that, they crossed the barrier and stepped into the dungeon. Witt wasn't sure what to expect. In all his time buffing heroes outside the dungeon, he had never been inside. He knew that by taking this first step, his destiny was about to change.

When his foot touched the first stair, his new life began. With his lute slung across his back, he gripped his twin daggers tight.

Hux stepped through without pause. He didn't seem nervous at all. Why would he be? He spent every day battling spiders on the mountain pass. He was no stranger to combat, but for Witt, dungeon diving was brand new. He wasn't scared, but he didn't know what to expect.

Torches adorned the walls as they descended deeper into the dungeon. Their flames gently cracked in the damp and musty air. Somewhere in the distance, water dripped methodically.

Drip. Drip. Drip.

The kobolds' claws clacked against the stone floor with each step.

The stairs emptied into three long corridors, with one to the left, center, and right. Torches once again lined the walls, but as far as Witt could tell, there was no real way of knowing which way they should head.

"Which way should we g—"

A scream and clash of metal down the hallway to the left cut off Witt's words. Hux nodded and they both set off in the direction of the clamor. The closer they got, Witt could begin to make out voices.

"I need a heal."

"I just freaking healed you. Can you stay alive for five seconds without me babysitting you?"

"It's not my fault there's toxic goo on everything in this room."

"Will you two knock it off? Some of us are trying to —ugh—"

A stocky human wearing plate armor crashed against the wall about twenty meters ahead. The flames of the torches danced in the reflection of his armor as he sat there stunned. Blood trickled down from beneath his helm, painting his chestplate a dull red. A second later, a white light bathed him and the blood vanished. The knight crawled to his feet and disappeared back around the corner.

Witt activated his analyze skill and crept toward the corner. Hux followed close behind. They poked their heads into the room, careful not to be seen.

The first thing he noticed was the trail of ooze that covered the majority of the square room. The green gel glimmered in the torchlight.

When he spotted the source of the ooze, Witt took an involuntary step back, bumping into Hux. Panic flared through his chest and he jumped before realizing it was just the mage. He turned back to the monster.

Dire Snail
  HP: 253/400

The creature standing before them was the stuff of nightmares, even for a kobold. The giant snail was taller than the knight that challenged it. It slid across the stone floor like it was made of ice, wielding its barb-covered shell like a wrecking ball. The knight dove out of the way, his armor clanking against the stone.

Green sludge covered the gelatinous body of the snail, leaving a slimy trail everywhere it went. Bulbous eyes twitched like antennae at the end of two tentacles atop its head, each one staring off into different directions. Ridges and sharp barbs lined the gray spiraled shell that protected its vital organs.

When the knight slashed his sword, the snail retracted into the shell, gliding around, an unstoppable force of destruction.

The rest of the knight's party consisted of an elven mage and a human rogue. The mage wore a long flowing gown and carried a crystal scepter. Her blonde hair and gown had an ethereal glow to it, like a constant breeze followed her every move. When she walked, it was more like hovering an inch above the ground. The rogue clung to the corners of the room, only emerging to attack when the snail faced away from her. If not for Witt's darkvision, she would be hidden in the shadows. She was cloaked in black and armed with daggers that gleamed even in the low light.

The trio had whittled the snail's health almost halfway down, but at a cost. The knight's health was at fifty percent, even after the heal. The rogue had lost a third of her health despite hiding in the shadows. The mage was the only one not hurt, but judging by her health bar, a stiff wind could take her down.

The snail came to a stop against the wall with a gentle thud and emerged from its shell. The knight charged in, but this time the snail didn't recoil. It raised its head high in the air, revealing a set of jagged teeth that hid underneath its belly.

An ear-splitting shriek poured from its mouth, freezing the knight in his tracks. As he stood there frozen, the room shook violently. Panels in the ceiling opened and giant globs of jelly fell into the room below, landing against the stone floor with a splat.

"Oh, you've got to be kidding me!" The rogue shivered.

Witt analyzed the substance, immediately realizing it wasn't a substance at all, but more monsters.

Dire Slug
HP: 100/100

The slugs had barbed ridges that ran down their spine, and sharp pincers capable of causing immense pain. They also radiated the same toxic goo as the snail. They swarmed the knight, who still stood frozen in place.

"Heal him!" the rogue shouted at the mage.

"I can't! My heal is still on cooldown. Get in there and help him."

The rogue shook her head and sighed before emerging from the shadows. For a moment, she looked like a shadow herself before attacking the first slug. Its HP dropped by fifty percent from the surprise attack. Half of the slugs immediately changed course, sliding toward the rogue.

The mage kept a safe distance, shooting darts of white energy from the end of her scepter. They sizzled as they hit the slugs, but didn't do much damage. Several slugs split off to chase the mage, but she moved with such grace that they could never get close enough to damage her.

While the rogue and mage battled the slugs, the dire snail moved in on the knight. It raised its head up even higher, mouth open wide as it descended on the knight. The knight's head and shoulders disappeared inside of the slug. Sharp teeth grated against armor as the dire snail attempted to devour the hero.

The stun wore off and the knight's arms flailed against the toxic underbelly of the beast.

A chill ran down Witt's spine and he found himself filled with glee. *Serves them right.* He glanced over his shoulder at Hux, who appeared equally amused.

The knight's health trickled down each second as he fought for escape. The rogue was now swarmed with more slugs than she could handle, and the mage was having little success in doing more than being a distraction.

The toxic goo ate away at the rogue with each step she took. Without the knight to tank the damage from the slugs, she wouldn't last much longer.

The knight's armor suddenly glowed a vibrant red, causing the snail to spit him out. Sludge covered him from head to foot, but it suddenly melted away. Flames coursed down his sword as he slashed at the snail before him.

The snail retreated and the slugs that had been chasing the mage honed in on the knight once again. His flaming sword cut through their bodies with ease, leaving them bisected and writhing on the floor.

Hux stepped closer. "Now is our chance. We must attack before they rally."

Witt gripped his daggers. The time had finally come. He analyzed the scene, trying to determine the best course of action. The knight was the toughest of the three, capable of taking more damage and therefore harder to kill. The rogue dealt the most damage, but she did it in bursts and was also more elusive. And then there was the mage; this particular one seemed to specialize in utility, not damage. If they could take her out and keep the others from being healed, then they would have better chance at survival.

Witt faced Hux. "I'll go for the mage. You go for the rogue. Then we finish the knight together."

He couldn't risk using his lute in this situation, so they would have to fight without the buff. Song and music would only draw attention to them.

Hux nodded. "Good luck."

Witt stepped into the room, careful to stick to the wall. The knight battled the dire snail, now wielding two swords, while the rogue continued to fight the slugs. The mage moved around the room, evading her pursuers and casting buffs as they became available. She raised her scepter and pointed it at the knight.

Now was the time to attack. He needed to disrupt her heal.

Flames burst to life across the room at the same time as Witt launched himself at the mage. He plunged both daggers into her back and the light from her scepter extinguished immediately. She screamed as he raked the daggers down her back, tearing through both flesh and clothing. Her health dropped by half from the attack. At level five, she wasn't much stronger than Witt.

"You..." Her face was full of shock as her words trailed off.

"Me," Witt snarled, stabbing another dagger into her midsection.

Blood stained her gown a deep red. She raised her scepter, hitting Witt with a bolt of white energy. It stung, but compared to what he had experienced at the hands of other heroes, it barely fazed him.

The rogue screamed in pain behind him, fueling his anger further. The mage tried to run, but she wasn't as elusive after taking so much damage. He stabbed again. And again. And again. Until her legs gave way and she tumbled to the stone floor. The toxic ooze finished the job, and Witt readied himself for his next victim.

His hands shook as adrenaline pumped through him.

The knight stood between the dire snail and Hux, a sword pointed outward in both hands. The flames no longer coated his blade and the aura had faded from his body.

"What is the meaning of this?" Panic coated his voice. "You were supposed to help us."

Witt laughed, and he surprised himself with how calloused he sounded. He joined Hux's side. The kobold mage's eyes burned with fury.

Witt smiled. "What's it going to be, us or the snail?"

The knight's helm shifted from the kobolds to the dire snail as he gauged his best chance at survival. Apparently, he thought he fared better against Witt and Hux, because he turned his back to the snail.

"It's no matter. I'll end you, then I'll clear this room and take all the loot for myself."

He spun both blades in a circle and marched on the kobolds.

Hux lifted his staff but before he could even cast a spell,

the dire slug lunged at the knight like a cobra, enshrouding him in its wide mouth. The knight disappeared in the belly of the beast and a moment later the snail coughed up bits of armor.

Hux burst out laughing, and Witt joined in.

"I can't believe that worked." Witt laughed.

"Well done, young Wi—"

A loud shriek echoed throughout the chamber, and Witt found himself unable to move. Armor clanked as the dire slug glided past the only remnants of the knight's presence. Hux's eyes were wide as the snail reared up, revealing its dagger-like teeth.

Witt watched helplessly as the snail swallowed Hux. He fought to move, but it was as if every muscle in his body had turned to stone.

Cool goo dripped down upon him as the snail hovered above his small frame. The inside of its mouth suctioned as its teeth spread wide.

Then there was darkness and pain. Witt's flesh ripped and burned, and then he felt no more.

CHAPTER TEN

Witt shivered. Being devoured by a dire snail definitely ranked near the top of the worst ways he had experienced death so far. Knowing he would respawn did little to ease the pain and discomfort when death came calling.

Once his heart quit pounding and the memory of his body being both shredded and burned simultaneously faded, Witt smiled. He and Hux had killed three heroes, and it had been an amazing experience. The back of his neck pulsed with frigid revenge. Killing the heroes had not dulled his desire to make them suffer. If anything, it had only grown stronger.

But what if they come looking for me? He quickly dismissed the thought. *I hope they do. Let them come to Murkwell and see what happens.*

The kobold image that was always floating in the top-right corner of his vision pulsed slightly. When he focused on it, the icon expanded into a sheet of parchment that hovered in front of him.

Notifications:

You have killed a level 6 hero.

You have killed a level 7 hero.

You have been awarded 2000 XP.

You have leveled up. You are now level 5.

You have leveled up. You are now level 6.

You have learned the ability Song of Swiftness (Bard).

Song of Swiftness: *Increases movement speed of those in the surrounding area.*

You have learned the ability Critical Strike (Barbarian).

Critical Strike: *Attack deals more damage but lacks precision.*

Due to your recent actions, you have been offered a new quest.

Quest: *Path to Villainy. By accepting this quest, you will embark on a journey to true villainy. Your power will only be limited by the atrocities you commit and the lives you ruin.*

Witt froze. Partly due to the shock of reading the prompts before him and partly due to the ice settling in his veins. His eyes focused on the last prompt. *Path to Villainy.* This was it. His days of being a simple skald were over. He had the chance to be a truly great kobold. Not even that, a truly great villain. If he did this right, kobolds would be feared the world over. Their days of being knocked around and used as fodder would be done.

He accepted the quest and another prompt appeared.

Quest Alert: *You have accepted the quest Path to Villainy. Due to your recent actions, you have gained a negative reputation among heroes and are now known as The Killer Kobold. Heroes will be offered a reward for killing you on sight. You have been awarded 50* *villain points (25 per hero killed) and will lose 25 every time a hero kills you. Upon reaching zero villain points, you will lose your reputation and your path to villainy will be over. For every 100 villain points you acquire, the bounty on your head will grow, increasing the threats on your life. Due to your low villain points, you may still travel in relative anonymity unless you are actively engaged in villainy or are recognized by a hero.*

Quest Alert: At 100 villain points you will gain influence over your fellow kobolds. Acquire 100 villain points to unlock additional options.

A calmness washed over Witt. *The Killer Kobold.* He smiled at the moniker. As far as villains went, it wasn't a bad name. He glanced over the rest of the prompts. There was so much to process in the quest alerts and notifications that he didn't know where to begin.

The one thing he was certain of was that he needed to gain one hundred villain points. That was priority number one. Witt had witnessed the power that Inspired Frenzy had on his fellow kobolds, but if he could influence their direct action or convince them to join his cause, then there would be no stopping his rise to power.

He would have to be smart. With only fifty villain points, two deaths could end his adventure before it even began. He needed to find Hux and plan their next attack.

He wondered if the heroes operated in a similar fashion. Did they receive hero points or did they level up based solely on experience gained from killing things?

Witt noticed that his stat page had updated with his new levels and abilities, as well as a few new rows for his title and alignment. His stat points had also increased in both Intelligence and Charisma.

Name: *Witt*
   Title: *The Killer Kobold.*
   Race: *Kobold*
   Class: *Skald (Barbarian/Bard hybrid)*
   Level: *6*
   Alignment: *Chaotic Evil*

STRENGTH: *10*
   DEXTERITY: *14*
   CONSTITUTION: *12*
   INTELLIGENCE: *9*
   WISDOM: *10*
   CHARISMA: *16*

Skills: *Darkvision, Perception, Languages (Common, Draconic), Pack Stratagem, Music, Lore.*

Abilities (available):

Skaldic songs: Only one song may buff a party at a given time. Affected allies must be able to hear the skald for the song to have any effect. Deaf creatures as well as undead, elementals, and constructs are not affected by songs.

1. Inspired Frenzy (bard): Increases Strength and Constitution of kobolds while sending them into a rage. Kobolds must accept the effects of Inspired Frenzy. Caster may also choose to accept the effects.

A raging song can be disrupted, and it ends immediately if the skald is killed, paralyzed, stunned, silenced, or incapacitated.

2. Strong Hand (barbarian): Hold a two-handed weapon in one hand.

3. Ballad of the Bold (bard): Increases Strength and Constitution of non-kobold allies.

4. Cleave (barbarian): Attacks deal splash damage in an arc.

5. Song of Swiftness (bard): Increases movement speed of those in the surrounding area.

6. Critical Strike (barbarian): Attack deals more damage but lacks precision.

Witt wished he could have more insight into what the future held for him. The ability to allocate his own stat points would have been a major advantage. As well as knowing what abilities he had coming, but there was no point in dwelling on the things he couldn't control. His life hadn't been easy so far. Why should that change now? He would have to work for everything.

But for once, he knew that he was truly doing good work. Work that would help his people gain the respect they deserved.

Witt grabbed his lute and crawled from his straw bed. Hux lived on the northern side of Murkwell and Witt needed to get there to see what shape the mage was in. He briefly recalled his own terror as his memories came flooding back during his fight with Stu.

He passed Zirn as the tinkerer was leaving the traproom for the day.

"Good day at the dungeon today, Witt?" Zirn's bulbous goggles stared him down.

"You could say that." Witt smirked. "I made a killing."

He nodded to Zirn and left the tinkerer as he navigated the maze of tunnels beneath Murkwell. Eventually, he found himself outside of Hux's burrow, only the mage was nowhere to be found. Witt ran up and down the tunnel, but there was no sign of Hux.

He hadn't passed the mage on his way here, so it was unlikely that Hux went out searching for Witt. *Where could he be then?*

Witt exited the burrow as twilight descended upon Murkwell. Many of the kobolds were preparing for a night of revelry. Food roasted over an open flame and three kobolds rolled a keg of kobold brew toward the fire pit.

Schekt rushed toward the keg, cup in hand. "Greetings, adventurer! Welcome to The Merry Minotaur, would you like a room or a drink?"

Witt shook his head and spotted Hux talking to Kessy out of the corner of his eye. Hux wore a confused look on his face.

"I can't remember the last time I missed my post for the day." Hux sighed. "Hopefully the heroes were able to fight off the spiders without me. Otherwise we will be in for a long night."

Kessy patted Hux on the shoulder. "I'm sure it will be fine. One missed shift won't be the end of the world."

Witt stood in silence. How was it that he was able to remember what had happened after respawning, but Hux couldn't? Then again, he had died many times and respawned without remembering. It wasn't until the traumatic experience with Stu, where the message "Don't forget" had been burned into his mind that he had remembered. Was that the key? Would he have to torture his fellow kobolds for them to remember their involvement with heroes?

If it came to that, Witt wasn't sure what he would do. But first he would try a simpler approach.

"Hux, how goes it?" Witt grabbed the mage on the arm and gave him a light squeeze.

"Ah, young Witt. Good to see you." Hux smiled." I am a bit out of sorts today. I overslept and missed my post. How was the dungeon?"

"You tell me." Witt gazed intently at the mage, looking for any sign of recognition.

Both Kessy and Hux scrunched their eyes.

"How would I know?" Hux shrugged. "I just woke up."

"You and I were just there together." Witt explained his trip to the mountain, where he flung himself from the side, his respawn, and their subsequent adventure into the dungeon.

At the end of the story, Hux stared at Witt, his face giving nothing away. Kessy, however, burst out laughing.

"Is this for a new song?" She pushed Witt in the arm, laughing. "I'm not sure how the heroes will react to a song about you killing them, but you're the skald, not me."

Witt frowned. *Of course, this would have been too easy. I'm afraid my only way to convince them is to die again.*

He took a deep breath. "Will you two follow me? I want to show you something."

Witt walked in silence, mentally preparing himself for what was to come. It would be painful, but he could think of no quicker way to get his point across.

They descended into the burrow, past Knoma's constantly

boiling stew, past the hatchery, and down the empty tunnel until Witt stopped in front of the traproom. Zirn had left and was somewhere above ground, probably readying the kobold cannon for a night of excitement.

"What are we doing down here?" Kessy stepped into the traproom and looked around.

"Just stand here." Witt pointed to the entryway. "I want to show you something. But no matter what happens, just stay here and wait. Everything will make sense very shortly."

Both Hux and Kessy looked at him with confused expressions.

Zirn's new glass projectile contraption was still situated in the middle of the room. Witt had witnessed its destructive power and was careful not to accidentally activate it before he was ready. Carefully, he moved the wooden block topped with a bloodmelon out of the way and stood behind the trap tile.

"What we have here is Zirn's newest invention." He winked at the duo by the door. "Enjoy the show."

Witt took a deep breath and stepped on the tile. In an instant, the tile gave way, activating the button and triggering the trap. There was an explosion of pain as the glass projectiles pierced his skull, and just as quickly, it was gone.

CHAPTER ELEVEN

Witt climbed out of his bed and rushed down the tunnel. He found Hux and Kessy huddled over the trap that had exploded his face only moments before. There were no traces of his body, but the broken glass from the projectiles littered the floor.

"Ahem," Witt coughed loudly.

Kessy looked over her shoulder and gasped.

"Mother loving frost giant!" Hux exclaimed, pointing his staff at Witt. "Is this some kind of illusion? Explain yourself, Witt."

Witt walked calmly into the room, hands raised. "This is no illusion. You just witnessed my death and respawn. This is the same reason why you woke up thinking you missed your shift in the mountains. The only difference is that for some reason, I am able to remember my deaths while the rest of you respawn with no knowledge." Witt paused to let the words sink in. "It's like every day we wake up with no memory of our interactions with the heroes."

"Why?" Kessy's voice was barely more than a whisper.

"I think this is some kind of game to them. And now it seems I'm a part of it."

Hux scratched his chin. "What do you mean?"

Witt explained to him his notifications and his villain points, how he had been killed relentlessly, and how if he killed more heroes he would become stronger.

Hux sighed. "And every day you will wake up with this knowledge, while the rest of us will have no memory."

Witt nodded. "I believe so. I had hoped you would remember our fight in the dungeon when you respawned, but it wasn't to be. So for the time being my only way to convince you is by killing myself and going through this process all over again."

Hux paced back and forth. "There has to be another way."

"Well." Witt pulled up his notifications again. "If this quest notification is true, then when I have one hundred villain points, I'll be able to influence other kobolds. This may mean you will help me fight the heroes without me having to prove that they are evil each day."

Kessy clapped her hands together. "Then what are we waiting for? Let's go kill some heroes."

Witt smiled. Kessy had always been an adventurous spirit. She'd support Witt no matter what.

"Just the three of us?" asked Witt.

Hux wore a pensive expression. "If you and I were able to kill three heroes on our own, then with Kessy we should be fine. It is nearing nightfall and most of the heroes will be retiring for the night. If you want to do this tonight, I don't think we have time to convince any of the others to join us."

Dammit! Hux was right. It was almost nightfall and the city gates would be closing soon. No one was allowed in or out of Skullheyden after dark unless they had a good reason. If they wanted to kill a hero tonight, they would need to find someone traveling to the castle.

"We need to hurry." Witt had been locked out of the city before and forced to travel around the castle walls back to Murkwell. To get to where he wanted, they would have to pass through the city first. "I have the perfect idea, but we need to leave now." It had been fun to backstab the heroes in the dungeon, but for his first act as a true villain, Witt wanted a little poetic justice. He was a skald after all.

Hux and Kessy walked toward the tunnel when Witt stopped them.

"Wait, I have a new song that should help get us there faster."

He'd unlocked Song of Swiftness after killing the heroes in the dungeon. Once he played the song, it would buff those surrounding him with bonus movement speed.

He strummed his lute and focused on his new song. Power rose up inside of him, like his insides were vibrating with each strum. Closing his eyes, he let the words come to him.

"Hugnu the Fleet, the Swift, the Bold,
Feared no man or beast, neither young nor old.
With lightning speed he roamed the land,
and gathered to him a merry band.
The kobold cause grew ever stronger,
and pure power was his only hunger.
As his army grew, so did his hunger,
until he could not wait much longer.
With thousands of kobolds by his side,
he marched on the city of Riverside.
They stormed the walls and took the castle,
aided by the kobold cannon..."

Witt continued the song of Hugnu, the first and only kobold king, who had taken the castle of Riverside and held it for two months before reinforcements arrived from neighboring kingdoms.

As he sang the song, fluorescent blue notes erupted from

Witt's lute with tremendous speed, dissipating into both Hux's and Kessy's bodies. When either of them moved, it was as if a breeze followed in their wake.

"Wow." Kessy took a few steps, her legs moving more rapidly than they ever had. "This is amazing."

Witt finished the Song of Swiftness and a gentle gale engulfed all three kobolds. He slung his lute across his back. "To the Pit of Despair!"

They rushed down the tunnel. When they emerged from the burrow, the sun nearly touched the horizon. They would need to hurry to make it through both city gates and to the Pit of Despair.

"Greetings, adventurer! Welcome to the Merry—"

"Not now, Schekt!" Witt cut off the kobold bartender. "We have business to attend to."

As they raced across Murkwell, several kobolds glanced in their direction. The trio undoubtedly looked out of place moving at such a rapid speed and leaving a breeze in their wake.

Before long, they were at the northern entrance to Skullheyden. A handful of guards stood sentry. They eyed Witt suspiciously but didn't stop him. His villain points weren't high enough to bring out their scrutiny. *Not yet,* he smirked.

He took in the city as they raced through it. One day soon, he would no longer be allowed within its walls. Once he became a true villain, he would need to find his own fortress. There would be many heroes interested in the bounty on his head.

The market was empty. All of the vendors had packed away their wares to return home hours ago. The shops were also closed. At this hour, only the taverns and inns showed signs of life.

They passed the Merry Minotaur Inn, where Schekt

worked during the day. Through the smoke-covered window, Witt could see a portly orc pouring drinks behind the bar.

Several heroes sat on the steps of a neighboring tavern laughing and talking of the day's adventures. How many innocents had they killed on their paths to gold and glory?

Witt's neck grew cool. They would get theirs in time, but it was too dangerous to attack them within the walls of Skullheyden.

A drunken dwarf stood up as they passed, finger pointed at Witt and the others. "Lookitthat!" His words slurred together.

Heads turned in their direction, but a moment later they were through the southern gate and out of Skullheyden.

"Gate closes in thirty minutes," one of the guards informed them as they left.

The road was fairly empty at this hour. The last of the city's population that worked outside the gates made their way in. Several heroes carried treasure, looking battered and beaten as they slogged by.

Witt fought the urge for the easy kill. He would have his vengeance his way.

Soon, they arrived at the Pit of Despair. The chasm cut through the earth about a mile from the entrance to the castle. At the bottom of the pit, molten lava bubbled and splashed a vengeful orange. Hot dry air constantly drafted upward.

Legend said that the first dragons had risen from the pit's heated depths. The pit itself was more of a roadside attraction than anything. Many would journey to the pit to toss items into the lava below. Some viewed it as luck, while others harnessed its destructive powers to destroy cursed items. It was one of the few places in the surrounding area that had such power.

Witt had suffered his own destruction in the pit when a

minotaur had thrown him over the edge. His skin had blistered and peeled long before the lava snuffed the life out of him. The memory sent a jolt of frozen lightning down his spine.

He motioned for Hux and Kessy to join him behind a boulder near the edge of the pit. In the twilight, the boulder's shadow concealed their small forms from view of the road.

"What now?" Kessy knelt beside him.

"Now we wait."

Minutes passed and still no one passed by. The sun dipped closer and closer to the horizon until the only light came from the moon overhead and the lava below. The glowing eyes of Skullheyden Keep watched them ominously above the city walls.

"Maybe tonight isn't our night," offered Hux.

Witt refused to believe that. There were always last-minute stragglers everywhere. The entry to the city would be no different.

Something clanked in the distance and Witt's heart leapt.

"Dude, we need to hurry or we won't make it to the inn." A shadowy form ran down the road, too far away for Witt's darkvision to reveal their features.

"Just let me toss this into the pit. I'll complete my quest and have enough to buy new items in the morning." A second, more portly figure brought up the rear.

"Bro, I don't think we have time." A third shadow hobbled along.

"Come on, I'll pop a movement potion once we're done."

"Dude, seriously? You've had a movement potion this entire and didn't think to use it."

As they got closer, Witt could finally make out the three heroes. One was a short and pudgy human paladin. His dull gray armor clanked with each step. If not for the stat screen detailing his race, Witt could have easily mistaken him for a dwarf. Beside him, two halfling rangers waddled on their short legs, trying to keep up. One held a bow, the other a crossbow and a whip.

The paladin came to a stop near the edge of the pit. He unhooked a satchel that was tossed over his shoulder and placed it on the ground. "Here, help me carry this thing to the edge."

The paladin knelt over the satchel and loosened the opening. Witt had to do a double take when the paladin pulled out a chest that never should have been able to fit in the bag. Giant straps covered the chest, as if they were keeping it closed.

Once fully out of the bag, the chest shook violently.

"Mimic," Hux whispered. "Extremely dangerous and hard to kill."

The mimic continued to shake as it sat on the ground.

"Why are we tossing it into the pit again?" asked the bow-wielding halfling.

"I don't know. I think the hag wanted to destroy all evidence of its existence. Apparently, when a mimic dies, any items it has eaten pop out like loot."

"Why don't we just kill it and take the items?" asked the other halfling.

"Look at this thing." The paladin pointed at the mimic. "If these straps come loose, we're all dead. I'm lucky I even got this quest. Now grab a side and help me toss it in."

The paladin grabbed a handle on one side of the chest and the two halflings held the other. They seemed to struggle with its weight far more than when it had been in the satchel.

"Now is our chance," Witt whispered to his companions. "We sneak up behind them and push them into the pit."

Hux and Kessy both nodded.

Witt readied two of his barbarian abilities, Cleave and Critical Strike. Critical Strike would increase his damage, and

Cleave would grant him splash damage, magically hurting nearby enemies within a certain range.

The effects of Song of Swiftness had worn off, so the three kobolds crept silently toward their prey. The three unsuspecting heroes struggled to carry the chest to the pit's edge. They set the chest down, resting a moment before continuing.

When they lifted the chest again, Hux was the first to attack. A massive fireball exploded on the back of the paladin.

The chest fell from his grip, but before he had a chance to defend himself, Witt jumped on the paladin's back, burying a dagger into his neck. A wave of energy exploded from the attack, hitting both halflings and knocking them back.

Kessy plunged her pickaxe into the ribs of one halfling while Hux summoned a flame wall amidst all three heroes. The flames scorched through the leather straps that bound the mimic. With a snap, they broke free and the chest opened, revealing a set of monstrous teeth and a long writhing tongue.

Kessy jumped back in shock as the tongue wrapped around the halfling she fought. In a swift motion, the halfling vanished inside the chest along with Kessy's pickaxe. The mouth of the mimic closed with a thud and muffled screams echoed from inside.

"You're not gonna stop me from completing this quest!" The paladin elbowed Witt in the face, and blood spurted everywhere. The blow knocked Witt aside, and the paladin returned to the chest. He pushed with all his might, still attempting to fulfill his quest and toss the mimic in the pit.

Kessy hid behind Hux as the mage threw another fireball at the remaining halfling.

Witt focused on the paladin. He had nearly pushed the chest to the edge. Witt wiped the blood from his snout and readied his next attack. As the paladin heaved the mimic over the edge of the pit, Witt pushed him from behind. The paladin teetered on the edge before falling into the depths below.

The lone halfling stood with his back to the pit. He held his crossbow pointed at Hux. "Screw you! He completed the quest. You can go now."

Witt laughed. "You think we're here about the quest? Think again. We don't care about your little quest. We're not here for your items or your gold."

The halfling frowned. "If you're not here to stop him from completing the quest, then what do you want?"

"Vengeance."

Witt nodded to Hux and the mage unleashed a fireball, hitting the halfling square in the chest and knocking him over the edge.

Witt rushed to the edge to watch the hero plummet into the fiery depths when something wrapped around his leg with a snap. A surge of pressure pulled him off his feet and the next thing he knew he was falling.

The halfling held onto the whip he had somehow managed to ensnare Witt with as he snarled. "If I die, you die."

A burning pain surged through Witt as they plummeted. The air grew hotter until each breath was painful. His eyes burned like they were melting from his skull. The last thing he saw was the outline of the kobold pulsing in the corner of his vision. Witt smiled as the heat consumed him.

CHAPTER TWELVE

Before doing anything, Witt pulled up his notifications. The pulsing image of a kobold expanded into a sheet of parchment before his eyes.

Notifications:

You have killed a level 7 hero.

You have killed a level 8 hero.

You have killed a level 7 hero.

You have been awarded 3000 XP.

You have leveled up. You are now level 7.

You have learned the ability Song of Silence (Bard).

Song of Silence: Prevents enemies from using abilities for thirty seconds.

You have been awarded 75 Villain Points. (x3 kills)

You have lost 25 Villain Points.

Quest Alert: *Bounty. You have reached 100 Villain Points and now carry a bounty on your head. At 100 Villain Points, heroes who see your face will recognize you as The Killer Kobold. For every 100* *villain points you acquire, the bounty on your head will grow, increasing the threats on your life.*

Witt let out a low growl of pleasure. They'd managed to kill three heroes. Even though he had died, he'd still earned enough villain points to unlock the next stage of his quest. Not to mention the new ability, Song of Silence, could effectively shut down the heroes' abilities for half a minute. A stat point had even been added to his Charisma.

All in all, Witt's life was looking up.

Hux and Kessy would likely have to take the long way home, but considering everything he'd unlocked, it was well worth it.

Witt pulled the notifications back up. He'd only glanced over the final notification.

Quest Alert: *For acquiring 100 villain points, kobolds from the village of Murkwell will be sympathetic to your cause. They will be more inclined to offer help in your rise to villainy and attack heroes on your behalf.* **Warning:** *Kobolds who die as a direct result of your quest will not respawn, but instead will reincarnate in the form of an egg in the hatchery.*

Witt frowned. On the one hand, he now had the support of his village. On the other, if any kobolds died because of his quest, they were gone for good. If Hux died in a dungeon, the village would be out its only mage, and there was no guarantee the next egg to hatch would be another mage.

He'd never mourned the death of another kobold before. Death was the end, but also a new beginning. However, now that he knew they could respawn, that they didn't have to truly die, life felt different. The only way Witt would lose his friends was if he screwed up.

His actions could very well change the fate of Murkwell forever.

Since it would be a while before Hux and Kessy returned, Witt went aboveground to enjoy the festivities and celebrate his good fortune.

The moon broke through the trees overhead, casting the village in a silver glow. Since kobolds had darkvision, there wasn't a need for torches on most nights unless the clouds were especially heavy. The only flames came from the fire pit where meat sizzled on a spit, and the occasional streak of glory as someone launched from the kobold cannon.

"Greetings, adventurer!" Schekt stumbled into Witt, sloshing his drink and spilling a hefty amount on the ground. "Welcome to The Merry Minotaur, would you like a room or a drink?"

Witt rolled his eyes. "You're such a sloppy drunk. You know that, right?"

"Greetings, adventurer..." Schekt continued, but Witt left him to his drunken stupor. He had too much on his mind to put up with Schekt's drunken antics.

He found a boulder between two trees and climbed on top. From where he stood, he had a decent vantage point of the nearby area. For a moment, he took it all in.

Young kobolds ran around the fire, tossing twigs into the flames and watching the embers rise into the sky like fireworks. The elder kobolds sat on logs, drinking and gossiping. Gragar, one of the oldest kobolds, occasionally lifted a gnarled finger and pointed it at someone without regard. The young farmers and miners were always engaged in some act of competition, testing their prowess with wooden weapons they would likely never use.

Witt scowled. *Likely would have never used. Things are about to change. Pretty soon you'll all have a chance to make a name for yourselves.*

Something moved in the shadows nearby. Witt focused on the blotch of darkness, but even with his darkvision, it remained hidden.

Witt's pulse raced. Was it possible one of the heroes had tracked him down already? He'd only just became a villain. How would they know where to find him?

His hand slipped down to the dagger strapped to his leg. The cold steel was icy to the touch.

The shadow crept closer, and Witt gripped the dagger tighter. He readied Critical Strike and a rush of energy surged down his arm until the dagger vibrated beneath his touch.

The shadow pulsed and a dark figure leapt toward Witt. Witt raised his dagger and slashed in front of him.

The figure ducked, and then laughter echoed through the forest.

"I'm surprised you saw me." The shadows faded, revealing a ruby-red kobold wearing a dark leather tunic. Red scales faded to black around his snout, making his teeth appear even more dangerous.

Witt let out a sigh of relief. He sheathed his weapon and flashed a smile. "Razul, you son of a dragon, I haven't seen you around these parts in ages."

Razul was a kobold rogue who spent most of his time living in the city. The quests he performed inside Skullheyden were another source of income for the village.

He climbed onto the boulder next to Witt, and slapped him on the back. "I just finished up a quest. Tomorrow I'll be leaving with a caravan of heroes bound for New Hope Cove. I figured I would stop by and say goodbye to everyone. This one will be a difficult journey and I'll be gone even longer than last time. How's life at the dungeon?"

Heroes. Witt's mind raced. This could be another opportunity to increase his notoriety. If he could somehow manage to kill an entire caravan, then he—

"Witt? You in there?" Razul poked him in the shoulder, interrupting his thoughts.

Witt turned to face Razul. "Yeah, I'm good. I'm no longer working at the dungeon. Let's just say I've expanded my horizons. Tell me about this caravan."

Razul cocked an eyebrow. "No longer working in the dungeon? Is young Witt moving up in the world?"

Witt grinned. "I'll tell you my story, but first I want to hear about yours."

Razul ran his tongue across one of his incisors. "Consider me intrigued. I'm a part of a crew hired to accompany a group of heroes to New Hope Cove. I don't know all of the details, but apparently whatever is happening in the cove is more than the heroes can handle on their own. It should be a nice bit of coin for the village." He leaned forward and placed a hand on Witt's shoulder. "Now, tell me, what is young Witt up to these days?"

Witt explained the past several days to Razul, detailing his interactions with the heroes, the deaths at their hands, and his new quest to become a villain. When he was finished, he waited for the same shocked expression he had witnessed from Hux and Kessy.

Razul narrowed his eyes. "Those bastards, they will pay for this. I do not doubt that I have suffered egregiously at their hands myself." His claws scraped against the boulder. "The fire from the first dragons burns within us all. Gods help any heroes who choose not to remember that."

A cool sensation spread down Witt's spine. *This is it. I no longer have to convince them I am telling the truth.*

He'd always liked Razul. Sure, he was crass and a bit rough around the edges, but it took a certain type of intelligence to be a rogue. Especially one that didn't end up locked away beneath the castle.

Witt took a deep breath. "We need to destroy that caravan. Do you think you can delay them in the morning, so that we have time to set up a trap?"

Razul ran his tongue across his teeth. "It would be my pleasure, my treasure."

The cool sensation turned to ice. "Excellent, now what do you say we have some fun?"

Witt stood atop the boulder and readied his lute. Tonight was the perfect time to test out his abilities now that he was truly a villain. Now that he could influence kobolds beyond just the songs themselves, he wanted to see just how far he could push his powers.

He started with Song of Swiftness, and the fluorescent blue notes darted across the forest.

"Hugnu the Fleet, the Swift, the Bold,
feared no man or beast, neither young nor old.
With lightning speed he roamed the land..."

The notes zoomed through the trees like they were shot from an arrow. They exploded as they made impact with each kobold, and the resulting fragments dispersed into their bodies.

As Witt serenaded his people with his gravelly voice, they all began to move with increased speed. Children zoomed from their parents around the fire. Even the elderly kobolds moved with vigor.

Razul leapt from the boulder and a cloud of smoke followed in his wake. "Oh, this is good," he growled.

Witt finished the song and gazed at the village from atop the boulder. It was as if someone had sped up time as he watched kobolds scurry through the forest. His eyes followed Razul as he clung to the shadows of the trees. With Song of Swiftness buffing him, the rogue could be more deadly than ever. The last thing a hero would see would be a shadow of doom right before Razul stabbed them in the throat.

Cold glee spread through Witt's chest at the thought.

He strummed his lute again, readying the next phase of his plan. As the notes of Inspired Frenzy dispersed among the village, heads turned in Witt's direction. It was a tune they knew well, one that always captured their attention. Witt growled the words as he sang.

"In ancient times, when lands were young,
and dragons spoke the only tongue,
they ruled the lands and skies above,
and hoarded all the things they loved."

The eyes of the kobolds watching took on an eerie glow. Dozens of red eyes stared back at him. They swayed to the sound of the music, the buff from Song of Swiftness making their movements faster than normal. Had Witt not known the cause of their actions, it would have been unsettling.

When the song ended, several kobolds screamed into the night. Then more joined in. A shrill whistle cut through the crowd, quieting them, then Zirn's voice pierced the silence.

"Attack the troll!" he bellowed.

Snarls and growls answered the tinkerer's call to action. The community turned in unison toward the edge of the forest. Rage danced through them all. They were ready to destroy. As their feet pattered away, Witt called out.

"Wait!"

The forest froze at his command.

Every kobold stopped at once and turned toward Witt.

His heart pounded. Each kobold touched by Inspired Frenzy faced him, watching and waiting. Ice flooded his veins, and in that moment, he felt powerful. He could have taken

the kobold cannon, launched them over the walls to Skullheyden and torn the entire castle to the ground.

Witt unleashed a cold, maniacal laugh. "To the troll!"

The kobolds roared in response, and took off through the
moonlit forest toward the slumbering troll. Witt hurried after
them. He put his lute away and readied his daggers.

The group waited for Witt near the troll. Giant bubbles
of snot expanded and retracted from the troll's massive
nostrils with each breath. Tigra stood nearby with her
direweasels at the ready. Schekt held a cup in one hand and a
small sword in the other as he swayed back and forth. Razul
hid in the shadows of a nearby tree, almost invisible in the
dim light. Gragar, the elder kobold, leaned on a gnarled staff.

As Witt watched the elder kobold with his faded scales
and feeble body, an idea struck him. A thought that could
benefit the entire village. In his old age, Gragar provided very
little value to Murkwell. Knoma was elderly, but she still
cooked the best stew within a day's walk of the village. Truth
be told, Witt wasn't sure what Gragar did besides gossip.

His presence wouldn't be missed. A new egg, on the other
hand, held endless possibility.

Witt approached Gragar, and the elder's glowing red eyes
fell on Witt.

Witt placed a hand on Gragar's shoulder. "Gragar, you
have served the village faithfully for many years. You will have
the honor of dealing the first blow." Witt unsheathed a
dagger and placed it in Gragar's frail hand.

The elder stepped forward. He nodded to Witt and sham-
bled over to the troll. The elder kobold raised the dagger, and
brought it down upon the belly of the troll. The blade dug
deep, spilling blood and awakening the troll with a start.

The troll grabbed Gragar in its panic, and with a sickening
crunch, the life faded from the elder's eyes.

"Attack!" yelled Witt.

Kobolds descended on the troll, faster and stronger than ever before. Razul moved in an elegant dance of shadow and blood as he carved the troll from beneath. Tigra's direweasels bit and clawed.

The troll swung its arms violently, but Song of Swiftness kept the kobolds from its reach. Witt readied Critical Strike and landed a few blows himself. By the time the troll fell, they had only lost two kobolds in addition to Gragar.

All around him, kobolds celebrated their victory over the troll. Witt found Gragar's body and retrieved the dagger that the dead elder still held. He pried the weapon from Gragar's stiff fingers that held a surprising grip in death.

"Tomorrow, you begin anew. For as I rise, Murkwell will also rise."

CHAPTER THIRTEEN

Witt rushed out of his burrow the next morning, intent on catching Hux before he left for the day. He found the mage just as he emerged above ground.

"Witt, good fortune at the dungeon today." He tipped his staff to Witt and made to leave.

"Actually, we've got bigger plans and I need your help."

This time, when he informed Hux of his quest to become a villain and his interactions with the heroes, Hux accepted it without question.

"So you want to ambush the caravan?" Hux scratched his chin. "We can do it, but we'll need help. Let's go find Zirn."

They found Zirn in the traproom. Bits of bloodmelon lay scattered around the room. The trap that Witt had witnessed the other day was gone and a new contraption sat in its place.

Zirn's goggled eyes focused on Witt. "How can I help you?"

"We need traps, and we need them now."

Zirn's mouth curled into a smirk. "I like the sound of that."

While Witt filled in Zirn on his plan to ambush the caravan, Hux went to find a wagon. He returned a few minutes later with Olah and her domesticated boar. She was one of the village traders, and would make deliveries of kobold goods to the castle or other cities in the area. The boar wore a harness around its chest that attached to a wooden wagon. Zirn loaded the wagon with all manner of traps, powders, and equipment.

Thanks to Razul, Witt knew the direction the caravan would be traveling as well as where they planned to camp for the night. There was only one major road leading from Skullheyden to New Hope Cove. If Razul was able to delay the group's start, then they would be forced to camp in the open instead of reaching the inn. Song of Swiftness should give Witt and company enough of a boost to set up an ambush by nightfall.

As they set off down the tunnel, a commotion in the hatchery caught Witt's attention. He peeked around the corner and saw three young kobolds playing in the remnants of their eggs. The young kobolds looked at the pink fragments with wonder.

Two of the hatchery mothers watched after the young as they played. It was too soon to tell if the children had a magical class or if they would become laborers. For now, they had unlimited potential. Even if they became miners or farmers, they would still provide more for the community than Gragar.

Witt had no regrets about his decision. Rebirth had always been the way of kobolds.

Once above ground, Witt played Song of Swiftness. Zirn, Hux, Olah, and Witt rode in the back of the wagon as the boar zoomed toward Skullheyden.

Witt wore a cowl over his head as they entered the city.

Since he only had a hundred villain points, he wasn't infamous enough to draw the attention of the guards. But he wasn't ready to take any chances either. He'd made progress, but it could all be wiped out in quick order if he wasn't careful. He wanted his infamy to grow behind the scenes. Once he was powerful enough, then he would take center stage.

Thanks to the speed buff, they passed through the city just as the market was opening. Shopkeepers and vendors scurried through the cobblestone streets. A portly woman unloaded crates of eggs nestled in straw. An elf stacked mounds of delicious fruits sorted by color that glimmered in the morning sun. A gnome organized an assortment of oddly shaped mushrooms. Past the market, the shops were opening for the day. The smell of fresh baked bread wafted into the streets. A candlemaker flipped the open sign that hung from her window.

Heroes spilled out from the inns, ready to start the day's adventures. Witt caught a glimpse of Schekt as he entered the Merry Minotaur.

A large caravan waited outside of The Rusty Pickaxe Inn. The three-story inn had an actual pickaxe attached to the sign. A group of heroes crowded around the wagon in front of the inn, pointing and cursing.

"Someone sabotaged us!" A silver-haired elf in a flowing red gown pointed at a pile of wood littering the street around the wagon. "They broke the spokes on every wheel."

The wagon sat on the cobblestone, all four wheels broken and lying to the side.

Razul stepped out from behind the wagon. "Don't worry. I'll get someone to fix it, and we'll be on our way in a few hours. Go have a drink while I find someone to replace the wheels."

The elf shook her head and sighed. "Fine. I want to be on the road ASAP. Let's go grab a drink, boys."

The rest of the heroes followed her back inside the inn. Razul winked at Witt as they drove past.

So far, so good. That should give us plenty of time to get set up.

The clop-clop of the boar's hooves on the road sent Zirn off to sleep. His soft snores rumbled beside Witt.

They passed farms and forests as the countryside came to life, and Witt's mind wandered as they traveled down the pressed dirt road. Up until this point, whenever a kobold was involved in an action with a hero, they had no memory of it the next day. He wondered if that would change now that he had become a villain. He could already convince kobolds to join him with ease now that he had one hundred villain points. His quest was their quest in a way, especially those he recruited. So if they participated in his quest, would they recall what happened on this trip in the morning?

Time would tell. For the moment, the priority was stopping this caravan. Witt had counted at least five heroes, maybe more that hadn't been outside. There were also three non-heroes in their party. Razul, a gnome guide, and a minotaur warrior. If they killed all five heroes, that meant over a hundred villain points for Witt.

They would have to plan this carefully. Both Zirn and Hux were valuable members of Witt's team going forward. He couldn't afford to lose their skillsets. Sacrificing Gragar was one thing, losing a tinkerer or the only mage would be bad for Murkwell, not just Witt.

Hux leaned forward. "You're in a rare position, you realize that, right?"

"What do you mean?" Witt's situation was extraordinary, he knew that much, but he felt like Hux was getting at something deeper.

"You have an opportunity for greatness, to really elevate kobold society. Even if we have to play the villains to get there, our people deserve respect. I hope you do us proud."

Witt understood the sentiment. Even before his memories had returned, he never felt respected. Kobolds were pushed around and treated like nothing. Hell, they were treated worse than goblins. Only those with power like Hux were given the smallest amount of recognition.

Witt dug his nails into the wooden railing of the wagon. He would make them respect him, and if he couldn't do that, then he would make sure they feared him above all else.

The wind swept over them as Witt continually cast Song of Swiftness each time the buff expired. They received many astonished looks as they sped past wagons pulled by horses and the occasional group traveling on foot.

Olah pulled on the reins, bringing the wagon to a stop. The sudden change in momentum woke Zirn, and his magnified eyes were even wider than normal.

"Do you see that copse of trees up ahead?" She pointed to a small collection of trees in the distance. It looked like a miniature forest in a sea of plains. "That is where we should set up. The road passes through there. The inn they had planned to stay at is still many miles on the other side, so this is our best spot for an ambush. The trees will conceal us and keep the caravan from bypassing our traps. If Razul times this right, then it'll be dark when they pass through."

Zirn lifted his goggles and wiped the sleep from his eyes. "Yes, that will do nicely."

Witt agreed. There wasn't a better spot to lay siege to the unsuspecting caravan.

Olah pulled the wagon to the side of the road once they were inside the wooded area. There were enough trees, bushes, and vegetation that they wouldn't be seen until someone was already inside. Under cover of darkness, they likely wouldn't be seen at all.

Witt kept his cowl on as he worked, the cloth hood concealing his features. The road to New Hope Cove wasn't packed, but it still received a fair amount of traffic. He would need to keep his identity a secret for as long as possible.

Zirn let down the gate on the back of the wagon. "I'll handle the traps. I don't want any of you to accidentally kill yourselves by improperly loading a spring or a pulley. Witt, you and Olah can dig the pit in the road. That'll be the last line of defense if they try to blindly run past us. One of you dig while the other directs traffic. If anyone asks questions, we're on the king's orders." He handed Witt a small shovel. "Happy digging."

Zirn turned to Hux. "Hux, take these containers of boom powder and I want you to layer it across the road like fresh snow. When the time comes, a well-placed fireball will ignite it. Don't go blowing yourself up before we're ready."

Hux pulled a clay pot from the wagon and began spreading its contents across the road. Witt started digging. He wasn't used to manual labor, so his muscles quickly began to ache. However, he found that if he used Critical Strike with the shovel, then he could dig further with each movement. Even though his digs were less precise, it was more productive.

After a while he switched with Olah and took a break on the side of the road. After sending a knight in golden armor around their work zone, he took out his lute and played Inspired Frenzy. He gently stroked the chords and sang barely above a whisper.

Each note shot out from the lute, but they were weaker and slower than before. They swarmed Olah, dissipating into her body. Her eyes glowed red and she shoveled with increased vigor as a rage took over her body.

By playing softly, he could determine the range of the buff. The louder he played his music, the farther it would reach. While a rage was great for manual labor, Hux and Zirn needed their wits about them as they prepared the traps.

Olah dug furiously until the buff wore off, and then she switched with Witt. The day wore on. Occasionally, they navigated travelers around the pit they were digging. No one suspected them of foul play. Zirn had been right. Once they said that they were on the king's orders, no one questioned them.

By late afternoon, the pit was deep enough that Witt couldn't see the road above its edges.

"Excellent." Zirn nodded in approval. "Now I need you to sharpen stakes and bury them in the bottom. They won't be concealed, but the idea is that if the caravan tries to bolt past us, they won't be looking at the road as they try to escape."

An hour later, the pit was a death trap. The sun was nearly at the horizon. The time had almost come. Hux sat at the edge of the copse, watching the road for signs of the caravan.

Witt approached Zirn, who was up in a tree tying something to a branch. "What are you working on?"

The tinkerer's eyes lit up. "I'd hate to spoil the surprise." He made a few adjustments and then climbed down. "We test out traps all the time, but never on living subjects." He rubbed his hands together. "I can't wait to show these heroes some kobold ingenuity."

"What now?" Witt focused on the contraption Zirn had just finished tweaking.

Item. Projectile Netting. *When triggered, the trap will shoot a weighted net that entangles enemies.*

"Now, we wait." Zirn winked.

Zirn held onto a detonator that ran up the tree to the canister that held the weighted net. Witt noticed that there were nearly a dozen detonators strapped to Zirn's belt. Each one connected to a line that disappeared into the nearby trees.

"Are you planning on using all of those?" Witt wondered how Zirn could keep track of them all.

His lip curled up in a smile. "Only if we're lucky."

Olah sat near the wagon, peeling a potato and tossing it to the boar. Soon, it would be nightfall. A coolness crept over Witt at the anticipation. They'd had plenty of time to prepare. If they did this right, he'd be a stronger villain by morning.

Witt called to the group. "Alright everyone, let's go over the plan."

Witt's heart pounded when Hux gave the signal that the caravan was approaching. A chill crept across his shoulders, and the moon cast a silver glow over the covered wagon. Two large oxen pulled the massive caravan, and a gnome sat at the front holding the reins. He looked relaxed as they made their approach. There was no way to tell how many heroes hid behind the canvas covering.

From where Witt stood, he could see Hux and Zirn hiding in the depths of the bushes. His darkvision worked great in the moonlight. Olah was safe at the far end with her boar. She had served her purpose and there was no need to risk her life. The upcoming destruction would be best left to the professionals.

As the caravan entered the copse, Witt stepped from the trees and took his position in the center of the road. He strummed his lute and the strings glowed a vibrant white.

The gnome pulled on the reins, bringing the caravan to a stop. The oxen snorted and pawed at the earth for the sudden inconvenience.

"Out of the way, kobold!" the gnome shouted in a squeaky voice.

Witt took a slight bow. "As you wish. But could I interest

you in a buff for your journey? Perhaps one to make your travels quicker?"

"What's going on out there?" a female voice called from inside the caravan. Witt recognized the voice as the elf from earlier in the day.

The gnome peeled back the cloth flap to the inside of the caravan. "There's a kobold out here blocking the way. He says he wants to give us a buff to help us travel faster."

"This has been a miserable journey," a gruff voice answered from inside. "Pay him whatever he wants. I didn't sign up for a road trip. I'm ready for the adventuring."

The gnome released the canvas flap and turned to Witt. "How much for the buff?"

"For a great band of heroes like you? No charge." Witt smiled, the icy patch on his neck pulsing with ill intent.

"Very well. Get on with it." The gnome placed the reins in his lap and sat back.

Witt strummed the lute again and it flared with white energy as he began to sing Song of Silence. With each note, the lute grew brighter as Witt's words gained power.

"The world was dark and full of terror
for those who lived in the dragon era.
Blue, red, silver, and white,
no prey could hope to escape their might.
They burned castles and farms to the ground,
destroying families and razing towns.
And now the time has come again
for all to fear the dragon kin..."

As Witt continued to sing, the canvas flap parted and Razul climbed into the front of the wagon. In a fluid motion, he grabbed the gnome by the head and brought his dagger across his throat. Blood poured onto the gnome's tunic, soaking it a dark red while Razul muffled the gnome's screams. Just as quickly as he appeared, Razul vanished, letting the body slump over and leaving only a shadowy trail in his wake.

Witt finished the song, and with a final strum, the light that had built up inside of the lute exploded across the copse. It flared out like a saucer, expanding and then retreating back into the lute.

Startled shouts came from inside the caravan.

The female elf poked her head out. She screamed when she saw the body of the fallen gnome. "We're under attack!"

Click. Zirn activated one of his traps and the weighted net shot from the trees. The net entangled the elf, its weighted edges curling around her and pinning her to the seat on top of the gnome's dead body.

A dwarf and minotaur emerged from the back of the caravan. *Click. Click.* Two more traps activated. Poison darts zipped through the air from both sides of the road. Dozens of darts whizzed by. Cries of pain both inside and outside of the caravan echoed through the night.

"Enough of this!" The dwarf raised a metal staff into the air, pointing it in Witt's direction. A look of confusion painted his face as he raised the staff again. "What the hell? I can't cast my spells."

"Me neither," a voice echoed from inside.

"What's happening?" someone screamed in panic.

Click. A glass orb soared through the air, launched by some sort of miniature trebuchet. It cracked on the ground next to the wagon and a blue smoke engulfed the area.

"Now!" Zirn shouted to Hux.

A fireball appeared in the depths of the trees and soared toward the caravan. It hit the ground beside the wagon, igniting the boom powder.

The explosion was deafening. A wave of heat and energy knocked Witt off his feet as the powder exploded. The concussive force launched the caravan into the air, igniting the canvas walls and wooden frame. Tortured screams pleaded for escape from inside. Soon, they faded and the only sound was the crackling of fire.

Witt picked himself up on the ground. He basked in the warmth of the flames, but his insides were ice cold.

CHAPTER FOURTEEN

After a few minutes, the charred remains of the heroes and their companions dissipated into the ether. They would be respawning somewhere, likely in Skullheyden, and they would be pissed.

Zirn's eyes glowed menacingly in the night as his goggles reflected the burning caravan. The canvas had erupted into flames, leaving nothing but a scorched wooden skeleton. The oxen pulling the wagon had died in the carnage, and Witt's mouth watered at the smell of roasted meat.

He wondered if the heroes would know he was responsible for their deaths. None of them had spoken like they recognized him, and he hadn't revealed himself. Hopefully, he could keep his anonymity for a little longer.

The kobold image floating in the corner of his vision pulsed. A cold calmness washed over Witt as he pulled up his notifications.

Notifications:

You have killed a level 8 hero.
You have killed a level 8 hero.
You have killed a level 9 hero.
You have killed a level 10 hero.
You have killed a level 9 hero.
You have been awarded 5000 XP.
You have leveled up. You are now level 8.
You have leveled up. You are now level 9.
You have learned the ability Scale Mail (Barbarian).
Scale Mail: Scales gain increased damage reduction.
You have learned the ability Song of Enlightenment (Bard).
Song of Enlightenment: Increases intelligence and mana regeneration of allies.
You have been awarded 125 Villain Points.
Quest Alert: *You have reached 200 Villain Points. Kobolds within your party will now level up when participating in the Path to Villainy quest line. Your notoriety has also grown and the guards of Skullheyden will no longer grant you access to the city. Other cities remain unaffected.*
Quest Alert: *Due to your recent antics, you have also taken on the name The Cunning Kobold.*

Witt paused a moment to process all of the information. He now had a total of two hundred and twenty-five villain points. He'd also had a stat point added to both Charisma and Intelligence from leveling up.

The Cunning Kobold. His new moniker had a nice ring to it. Truth be told, their plan had been executed to perfection. They'd destroyed the caravan without taking any damage. Hux and Zirn would be invaluable assets going forward, especially considering the fact that they could now level up alongside him. Not to mention his new ability Song of

Enlightenment would likely benefit both of them. Scale Mail, on the other hand, meant Witt might actually be able to get his hands dirty.

He focused on Hux, who was scouring the rubble of the exploded caravan. He was still level eight. So the experience points gained from their current wave of terror had only gone to Witt.

Next time. A wave of icy pleasure coursed through Witt. Soon, the villain points and experience would be flowing like a waterfall.

The inability to enter Skullheyden might be a problem. However, the notification said that the guards wouldn't grant him access to the city, not that they would kill him on sight. It was still possible he might be able to sneak in wearing his cowl.

That would be a problem for another time. The gates to the city were already closed at this point. They would be lucky to reach Murkwell by morning.

A shadowy figure moved through the bushes to Witt's right. He reached for his dagger and activated all of his barbarian abilities. His body vibrated with the unspent energy. Was it possible one of the heroes had escaped? Could there have been more than five in the caravan, or had one of their companions evaded death?

"Boo!" Razul's shroud faded, revealing his wild grin.

Witt jumped at the rogue's sudden appearance, and Razul tilted his head back in raucous laughter.

The tension fled from his shoulders. "Razul, you're a real piece of slime. You know that?" Witt couldn't be mad at the rogue. It had been his efforts that allowed them to ambush the caravan in the first place.

"I've been called worse." Razul shrugged. "That was quite the show. We should probably get going before anyone comes looking."

Witt agreed. The flames were a giant beacon in the darkness. He called Olah to bring her wagon over. "Let's take down these traps and load them in the wagon. We can talk once we're back on the road."

Since most of the traps had been used during the ambush, taking them down was a lot quicker than setting them up. Soon, they were on the road to Murkwell. He took one last glance at the dying embers of the caravan. *This is just the beginning.*

The night sky was clear and millions of stars sparkled overhead. For a moment, Witt sat in silence, listening to the crunch of dirt underneath the wagon. Today had been a great day. Razul sat to his right and Hux and Zirn sat across from him while Olah steered the wagon.

"Good job, everyone. We couldn't have executed that more perfectly." Witt leaned forward. "I have some good news. From this moment forward, for every hero we kill as a group, you will all grow stronger. Hux, you must have killed thousands of spiders in your days guarding the pass, and yet you're still level eight. Now, your efforts will be rewarded. And Zirn, I have a feeling we're going to need a lot more traps very soon."

The glowing moon reflected in Zirn's goggles. "More adventures like this, or are you planning something bigger?"

"I have big plans, but we must protect Murkwell from the heroes that will try to shut me down. The stronger I become, the greater the reward will be for killing me. We will need to keep our people safe, and the hatchery above all. It is our future." If the eggs were destroyed, then there would be no more kobolds in Murkwell.

Zirn nodded. "Consider it done. I will make sure all of the other tinkerers return to Murkwell as well."

"And Hux." Witt turned to the mage. "If we want to do

this, I mean really do this, then we are going to need to get stronger. And fast."

Hux scratched his chin. "It is quite the predicament. The more heroes we kill, the more they will want you dead. How do we grow stronger without attracting attention?"

"Leave that to me." Witt had a sprout of an idea growing. One that could level up his people right under everyone's noses.

Razul used his claws to flake off specks of blood that stained his leather tunic. "I hope you will have use for me, now that I will most likely no longer be welcomed in Skullheyden."

"We couldn't have done this without you. Your talents will become extremely valuable in the coming days. Don't you worry." Witt smiled.

He pulled out his lute and began to sing Song of Swiftness. The notes jumped from the lute, igniting the night as a gentle breeze engulfed the wagon. They sped along the empty road. It was a rarity for people to travel the roads at night, with the towns and villages closing their gates at sunset. Only outlaws and ne'er-do-wells roamed the darkness.

And villains. Witt basked in his new title. He was well along the path to villainy, and nothing would stop him now. As the wagon bumped along, he and the others drifted off to sleep. In a few hours, someone would switch with Olah so that she could rest.

"Witt, wake up." Olah's voice was coated with urgency as she shoved Witt's shoulder.

He wiped the sleep from his eyes. "Ungh. Is it my turn to drive?"

The wagon moved at a snail's pace, the buff he had given

long worn off. Hux, Zirn, and Razul lay fast asleep next to him. The moon had disappeared behind the clouds, and no longer cast the fields in a silver hue. The pressed dirt crunched underneath the wheels.

Something was wrong. They were barely moving at all.

Olah shook Witt again. "Wake the others. There is someone on the road ahead."

She pointed ahead to a wagon that blocked the road in the distance. Ravines ran on both sides of the road, making it impossible to go around. Several dark figures stood to both sides of the wagon.

Witt hurriedly woke the others. "Guys, I think we have a problem."

They stirred to consciousness. Hux and Zirn both looked worried. Razul cursed under his breath.

This was the exact reason no one traveled the roads after nightfall. Bandits were always searching for unsuspecting victims. *You picked the wrong wagon to ambush.*

"Stop the wagon," Witt ordered Olah.

She did as commanded and the boar came to a halt about fifty yards from the blockade. There was no guarantee they could turn the wagon around before the bandits ambushed them. The only way out of this situation was to go through them.

"Do we have any active traps we can use?" Witt's mind sprang into action. There was no way he was losing anyone to a group of bandits. He wasn't sure if this would count as part of his quest or not, so there was no telling if the others would respawn if something happened to them. He wasn't willing to risk any of their lives to find out.

Zirn shook his head. "The boom powder is all gone, and there's no time to set up the other traps, not when they know we are here. We may be able to use the poisoned darts and throw them by hand. I didn't use the ones coated with basilisk venom against the caravan."

Witt sighed. "Okay, I'll see if I can talk our way out of this." He did have a seventeen in Charisma after all. "Razul, sneak out of the wagon while I distract them. If we are forced to fight, we'll need the element of surprise."

"Here, take this." Zirn scrounged through one of the containers and handed Razul a handful of darts. "Be careful. The poison causes temporary paralysis."

Witt moved to the front of the wagon and stood on the seat. He bowed to the bandits. "Greetings, travelers, are you broken down? We're but a lowly group of kobolds, but perhaps we could offer assistance."

Witt seethed as he said the words. He was a villain now, and groveling was beneath him. But if it got his people out of this safely, he would defer his fury for now. He doubted it would work, but at least he could say he tried. There was a reason the gates stayed locked at night.

A cloaked individual stepped forward. "It's awfully late for a group of kobolds to be on the road. Shouldn't you be tucked away in your burrow?"

Several others laughed at the comment.

Witt did his best to play the lowly kobold. "Oh, you know how it goes. Us kobolds get stuck with the jobs no one else wants. We were tasked with transporting troll dung down to New Hope Cove. We're just trying to make it home before morning."

"New Hope Cove, eh? Isn't that where the regional event is unfolding? They say a golden dragon has awakened in the mountain. I hear..."

Witt zoned out at the mention of a dragon. It had been years since someone had last spotted one. It couldn't be a coincidence that the dragon appeared at the same time Witt began his path to villainy. This was a sign. And just like a dragon, Witt would show no mercy.

"Let us take a look in your wagon and we will let you live." The hooded figure continued. "Deny us, and this is the last night you'll ever see."

Out of the corner of his eye, Witt noticed that Razul had disappeared. Good. Now he just needed to find out how many bandits they were up against. There could be more hiding behind the wagon.

Witt climbed down from the wagon. "Be our guest."

The others joined Witt, taking several steps back as the bandits approached.

The figure laughed. "And here I thought kobolds were stupid."

A chill ran down Witt's spine, and he fought the urge to reach for his dagger. Four figures in similar garb pulled up the rear, leaving their own wagon unattended. Perhaps this wouldn't end in violence after all. What were a few lost traps in exchange for their safety?

Witt tapped Hux on the shoulder and pointed toward the bandits' wagon. If they could make it to the other wagon, then perhaps they could escape before the bandits knew what was happening. Hux nudged Olah and Zirn in the arm and nodded his head in the same direction.

As the bandits moved closer, they appeared even more threatening. The leather armor they wore was studded around the breast and shoulders. Each bandit wore an assortment of daggers and knives strapped to their bodies. By the look of them, they weren't magic casters. If they had been, they likely wouldn't be on this empty stretch of road. No, these were bullies.

Witt clenched his fist. They were no better than the heroes.

"Keep an eye on the kobolds," the leader ordered.

Two bandits pulled their swords and pointed them at Witt and company.

"There's no need for that," Hux objected.

"What? You think we're going to let you crafty kobolds attack us unaware—"

The leader froze in place.

"What the he—" There was a slight thunk before a second bandit stood motionless.

The remaining three turned in unison just as three more poisoned darts pierced the leather armor in quick succession, paralyzing the bandits.

Razul popped out from the shadows still holding several darts. He lifted one and examined it. "How long does this stuff last?"

"We've got a few minutes before it wears off." Zirn walked over and kicked the closest bandit in the shin. "They can still feel pain, but they can't move."

Razul snarled. "We should gut them where they stand."

Witt climbed on the wagon and stood in front of the leader. "I like your thinking, Razul, but I have a better plan."

He lifted the leader's hood, revealing the bandit's face. Wide eyes stared back at him. They pulsed with fear as they followed Witt's every movement. The man's face was plain except for a scar beneath his right eye. Shaggy brown hair dangled across his forehead.

"Crafty kobolds, is that what you called us?" Witt pulled his dagger and pressed the cold metal to the man's face. "I think you meant *cunning*." He leaned in close, whispering into the man's ear. "Remember the day that I showed you mercy. When you are ready to become more than a simple bandit, come find me." He kicked the paralyzed bandit and the body fell to the ground with a crunch. "Razul, you and I will take their wagon. Olah, follow close behind."

They climbed into the bandits' wagon. Razul took the

reins and whipped the horses into action and they set off at a quick trot.

Witt stood in the back of the wagon, lute in hand. As they disappeared down the road, the crumpled bodies of the bandits began to stir. "Not bad. Not bad at all."

He strummed the lute and sang Song of Swiftness, buffing both wagons with added speed.

"Can I ask you something?" Razul looked over his shoulder.

"What is it?"

"Why let them live? They would have killed us without thinking twice. They probably would have killed us after looting the wagon if we hadn't been prepared."

Razul was right. They probably would have killed them, but Witt was thinking about the long game now.

"You're right. But now the last thing he thinks about every night before falling asleep will be the cold iron of my dagger pressed against his cheek. He'll know that I could have killed him. I could have taken everything from him, but I showed mercy. He'll never let his guard down again, and then one day, he'll thank me for it."

CHAPTER FIFTEEN

The wagon pulled into Murkwell just as the sun began to peak above the mountains. The group had rotated driving throughout the night, so Witt had enough energy to jump into the day. There would be no rest for the wicked, and he was feeling exceptionally villainous. Olah's boar, on the other hand, snorted and huffed every chance it got.

Several kobolds scurried around the village, already on their way to work.

"Witt, what's going on?" Kessy stepped in front of the wagon, a pickaxe slung over her shoulder. "I missed you at the fire last night."

Witt climbed down from the wagon. "It was a crazy night. We killed a few more heroes, outsmarted some bandits, and stole their wagon." He enjoyed the shocked expression that overtook Kessy's face. "Murkwell now has its first pair of horses." He pointed to the wagon Razul was driving.

Kessy tilted her head, mouth hanging open, before finally speaking. "You did what now?"

Witt grinned. "I'll explain everything shortly. Can you

help gather everyone aboveground? I have an announcement to make."

She scrunched her eyes. "Uh, sure. Give me a minute."

He turned to his party. "Hux, Zirn, could you help her gather everyone? Razul, help Olah put the wagons away."

Everyone jumped into action. None of them so much as questioned Witt, either. Whether it was because he had won their respect with his actions or if it was a result of the path to villainy quest line allowing him greater influence over kobolds, he didn't know. He liked being in charge, though. It felt surprisingly natural.

Witt took a seat atop the giant boulder next to the fire pit and waited for everyone to show up. Slowly, kobolds gathered in front of him. They whispered among themselves, occasionally glancing in his direction. There was an electricity in the air. Things were about to change in Murkwell.

When Hux, Kessy, Zirn, and Razul joined, he strummed his lute, gathering everyone's attention. A familiar coolness washed over Witt as all eyes fell on him.

"Thank you for gathering here this morning. I know many of you are anxious to get to your posts for the day. Do not worry, I'll keep this brief, but it is of great importance to all kobolds, for I intend to change our very way of life."

Whispers snaked through the crowd. He waited for them to die down before continuing.

"It's no secret that kobolds have been the laughingstock of society for ages. Once we were respected. Our ancestors were born of the same fire that the first dragons crawled from to shape the world. Now, we find ourselves lower than the green-skinned vermin they call goblins. Sure, some of us have risen to prominence like Hux or Zirn here, but even they have suffered. Orcs, humans, dwarves, elves, it makes no matter what race they are, they treat us like we are nothing.

They use us to mine, to farm, to keep their cities prospering, but they do not respect us. The heroes treat us worst of all."

Several kobolds gasped at the last line.

"Yes, for too long we have served the heroes thinking that they were the saviors of the world. Because they complete quests, clear dungeons, and battle monsters. The truth is that they are the monsters we should be battling. They are not our saviors. I do not doubt that every one of you has suffered at their hands. Up until now, the cruel injustice of the gods has kept those memories from you. Today it ends, because I am done being a plaything of heroes, and it is high time they learn that kobolds have our hands all over this world. And if they don't watch out, we'll tear it all apart!"

He strummed his lute again. Kobolds hissed and roared as Witt lifted his fist into the air. His newly gained points in Charisma must be paying off, because he had never seen them so enraged outside of Inspired Frenzy.

He'd won them over without having to tell them of the many deaths he'd experienced. He no longer had to justify his actions to have the support of his people. Looking out at the crowd before him, Witt had his very own army. Now, he just needed to learn how to use them. Taking a small group to ambush an unsuspecting caravan was one thing. Leading an entire village was quite another. His responsibility had always been to the village, but now the village itself was his responsibility.

"That is all for now. Go to your posts and keep a vigilant eye on the heroes you encounter. They must not suspect that we know their true motives. Tonight, I will have more information."

The crowd dispersed and Witt joined Hux and the others. "It's time to start defending Murkwell. Zirn, we need all the tinkerers you can find. Kessy, we need laborers. Pull a handful of miners and assist Zirn with setting traps. Razul and Hux, meet me in my burrow. I have plans to discuss."

As everyone dispersed, Kessy grabbed Witt by the shoulder and pulled him aside. "What's going on?"

"What do you mean?" He thought he'd explained pretty well what was happening.

"Something has changed. I can't quite put my finger on it, but... you've changed. It's like I'm inclined to believe everything you say without questioning it." Her hand drifted from his shoulder to his chest, and she curled all her fingers except one, pointing the claw firmly against Witt's tunic. Her eyes shrunk to slits. "You know that's not how I operate. If the rest of them want to follow you like mindless goblins, then so be it, but I want answers."

Witt stared at Kessy. Somehow she was evading his influence. Was it because she was his oldest friend, or was there more at play?

"I've been offered a quest." Witt told her again of the heroes and his adventures since his reawakening. Her eyes went wide at the mention of their battle with the heroes at the Pit of Despair.

"I killed a hero?" She held a hand over her mouth.

"You did a pretty good job, too." Witt smiled.

Kessy laughed. "It sounds a lot more exciting than swinging a pickaxe all day. If it gets us some respect, then I'm all in. But no more secrets. If I'm going to help you with this, I want to know everything."

By early afternoon, Zirn had gathered four other tinkerers that worked in Skullheyden and brought them back to the village. They paired up with twenty miners hand-selected by Kessy and went about the defense of the village. By the time the rest of the community started returning for the evening, nearly half the entrances into Murkwell were laden with traps designed to capture, maim, and kill intruders. The traps grew progressively more deadly the further someone pushed into the village.

Scouts would supervise the traps at night in order to protect everyone while they were asleep. They would also be responsible for raising the alarm.

Witt hoped it wouldn't come to that. Things were still too new to put the village at risk.

He'd spent the day brainstorming his ideas for leveling up Murkwell with Hux and Razul. Tonight, they would put them to use.

As twilight came and coated the forest in the shade of night, kobolds drank and ate. Occasionally, one would approach Witt, informing him of the things that they had witnessed heroes doing. No one had seen a hero kill a kobold, but they were asking questions, specifically if anyone knew of The Cunning Kobold.

Word is traveling fast. Even more reason to lay low for a while.

Witt stood up, preparing to gather everyone's attention with his lute, when Cerent, the hunter from the neighboring village, came sprinting down one of the paths.

He came to a stop at the fire pit and leaned forward, hands on his hips as he gasped for air.

"What is it?" Hux rushed to his side. "What has you in such a fuss?"

"It's Swampside," Cerent panted. "It's under attack. They're burning our village to the ground."

"Who!?" Witt jumped down and grabbed Cerent around the arms, shaking him violently. "Who!?" He had a feeling he already knew the answer.

Kessy pried Witt's hands away. "Stop shaking him, and let him speak."

"It's the heroes. They said they were on a quest and if we didn't tell them who The Cunning Kobold was, they would kill us all. I couldn't make it into the burrow, so I came here for help."

Cold anger flared inside Witt. "Hux, Razul, come with me. The rest of you find safety. I want all of the traps set as soon as we leave."

Kessy stepped in front of Witt. "What about me?"

He placed a hand on her arm. "Keep everyone safe. I need to find out what is going on. Whatever you do, don't let your guard down. They could be coming here next."

Witt played Song of Swiftness as they ran. Swampside was on the other side of Skullheyden, closer to the Forgotten Quarters Dungeon, but if they cut through the forest it would save them close to an hour.

Due to Swampside being further from the mountain than Murkwell, their village provided more farmers and hunters than anything. Kobolds toiled in the fields for long hours harvesting the produce that many of Skullheyden's residents took for granted. Death to their workforce could have far-reaching ramifications.

Maybe you'll finally realize how valuable we are to society.

Witt's thoughts raced as they ran through the forest in silence. The bounty on his head must have grown in order to cause this. Most of the heroes might not know who he was yet, but they knew of his title. It seemed that was enough.

He could trust the kobolds of Murkwell not to reveal his true identity, but he wasn't sure if his influence affected those outside of his village. It was only a process of elimination before they descended on Murkwell as well.

The smell of smoke drifted through the air, and Witt slowed down. A fiery glow from Swampside cast the trees in an eerie light.

"Razul, take the lead. I want to know who is responsible for this."

The rogue nodded and stepped silently forward. His natural skills of evasiveness would offer them the best chance at sneaking up undetected.

The glow of the flames grew larger, and the crackle of burning wood filled the air. Muffled yells and the occasional crash of a falling building came from the distance. Razul kept to the shadows and Witt followed his every move.

A young kobold ran through the forest up ahead. She looked back over her shoulder and a moment later, a stumbling dwarf emerged from the bushes in pursuit.

"Get back here! I know you know where he is."

Witt's heart pounded. He recognized that voice. The black-bearded dwarf had been a part of Stu's party. He'd stood idly by and watched every time that Witt had been tortured and killed. His neck grew cool.

Of course, they were responsible.

Witt and company clung to the shadows as the dwarf rogue continued his pursuit. Witt wanted to go deeper into the village, but the opportunity for revenge called to him above all.

"Follow him," Witt whispered.

Despite being a rogue, the dwarf was loud and clumsy as he tracked the young kobold through the forest. This allowed Razul to follow him from a further distance.

Witt scowled at the bumbling fool. "He's a part of the dwarf party that killed me repeatedly. Now, it's our turn. The next time he stops, we take him out."

A moment later, the dwarf stood in a clearing, searching for signs of the young kobold. "Screw this. The reward is not worth this hassle."

He turned to go back to the village, and Witt stepped in his way.

"You!" The dwarf looked shocked. "Stu was right! It was you."

The dwarf lifted his crossbow and pointed it at Witt.

"Not so fast!" Hux erupted a wall of flame in front of the dwarf, obscuring his vision.

Razul pulled a dagger and his body faded into the shadows.

Witt debated between buffing his allies or going for the kill. An icy patch formed on the back of his neck and slowly crept down his spine. He wanted blood. Blood and vengeance.

He activated Scale Mail and Critical Strike and followed Razul's barely visible shadow. The sizzle of the flames concealed their movement as they flanked the dwarf from the side.

When the flames faded, the dwarf pointed his crossbow at Hux. "Where did he go?"

"Boo!" Razul revealed himself, startling the dwarf.

An errant crossbow bolt fired into the trees, and the dwarf panicked to load another one. But it was too late. Razul slashed at the dwarf's neck. The dwarf stepped back and the blade grazed his throat. A fireball exploded against his black leather armor, knocking him to the ground.

This is my time.

Razul went in for the kill, but Witt waved him off. "He's mine."

Witt lunged at the dwarf, his arm vibrating with the unspent energy of Critical Strike. The dwarf raised his crossbow, using it as a shield to deflect the blow. The passive energy of Cleave hit him with a wave of splash damage, dropping his health even though he hadn't taken a direct hit.

The dwarf thrashed, hitting Witt with the butt of the crossbow and knocking him aside. Scale Mail reduced the damage taken, but it still left him dazed as he crawled to his feet.

The dwarf grabbed at his neck where Razul had cut him. He scowled at Witt when he looked down at his blood-covered hand. "Stu was right. You stupid kobolds never learn your lessons." He tossed his crossbow to the ground and pulled out two daggers. "You want to fight? Call off your friends and let's fight."

Witt shook his head, the stars finally fading from his vision. He motioned for Razul and Hux to back off.

The whine of steel cut through the night and the dwarf clashed his two daggers together. He smirked as he looked down at Witt. "Your songs can't save you now."

Witt winked at Razul, and the rogue sprang into action. The rogue's body pulsed for a moment as he leapt at the dwarf, burying his own dagger in the dwarf's throat. The dwarf fell to his knees, holding both hands over the fatal wound.

Kneeling down in front of the dwarf, a calmness washed over Witt. "You want to know the difference between a villain and a hero?" The dwarf tried to speak but all that came out were gurgles. Witt leaned in closer. "I don't pretend to be something I'm not."

With three quick jabs, the life left the dwarf and he fell to the ground.

Something rustled in the bushes and all three kobolds turned, weapons raised. A tiny red arm peeled back the branches and a young kobold stepped forward, her eyes glistening.

She frowned. "Why are the heroes attacking us?"

Witt placed his hand on her shoulder. "They are not who we thought they were." He knelt down and looked her in the eye. "You can't trust heroes to look after us because they will always look out for themselves. We must do the same. Now, run to Murkwell, you will be safe there."

The young kobold took off toward Murkwell just as the dwarf's body began to dissipate.

When they reached the edge of Swampside, Witt's heart sank. All of their aboveground structures had been burnt to the ground.

A group of heroes surrounded a dozen kobolds that were tied up near the village fire pit.

"I'm not going to ask again. Which one of you is The Cunning Kobold?"

Fire and ice intertwined within Witt as the sound of the voice brought back his worst memories. Stu, the red-haired warrior dwarf who had caused him such pain, grabbed a kobold by the tunic.

There were at least seven heroes that Witt could spot. Three dwarves, an elf, a minotaur, a gnome, and an orc. As the light from the flames danced across their bodies, casting them all in moving shadows, they looked like the monsters they were. His nostrils flared as fresh anger surged through him.

"What can we do?" he whispered to the others.

Stu lifted the kobold off the ground by the tunic. The kobold's legs dangled in the air awkwardly.

"Is it you?"

"We don't know who it is. Whoever it is, they aren't from Swampside," the kobold pleaded.

"Liar!" Stu tossed the kobold to the ground. "Finch, show the others what will happen to them if we don't find out where this Cunning Kobold is."

The chocolate-colored minotaur stepped forward and without warning, brought a massive hoof down on the kobold's head with a sickening crunch. Hux and Razul averted their eyes, but Witt looked on, his hatred growing even stronger. His fist clenched around the handle of his dagger.

Hux placed his hand on Witt's shoulder. "I think we should leave. We can't save Swampside, but we can protect Murkwell."

Witt nodded. "You two go. I have business to finish, but I will see you back in Murkwell one way or another."

Hux gave him a questioning look, but he didn't argue. "See you soon."

Razul winked. "Good luck, young Witt."

And then they were gone.

One by one, Stu and the others killed the kobolds in brutal fashion. From spells to brute force, they inflicted pain and torture. Witt struggled with each death, refusing to look away. Every death was a kobold unlikely to respawn, their life force forever extinguished because the heroes were hunting Witt. He wondered how many kobolds hid in the burrows beneath the village, forced to sit idle while their brothers and sisters begged for their lives.

He pulled the lute from his back and plucked at the strings. While his barbarian skills had improved over the past few days, he was no match for the heroes before him. There were too many, and they were too strong for him alone. He looked over his songs, wondering if any of them might help.

Song of Enlightenment offered little in the moment. Song of Silence could stop the heroes from using their abilities, but the minotaur had proven that brute force was enough. With Song of Swiftness, the kobolds might be able to run to safety, but many would die in the process. Ballad of the Bold was useless. He had no intention of buffing a hero ever again.

That left Inspired Frenzy, the first song he had ever learned. The song that connected kobolds one and all, no matter if they were from Murkwell or not. It was a song of his people. A song for dragons.

Witt stepped into the burning remains of the village. He strummed his lute and the notes flared out, a rainbow of music finding its way to the kobolds restrained in the center, but also down the tight tunnels that led into the burrows underneath.

He sang with all the power he could muster, so that every kobold in the village would hear him.

"In ancient times, when lands were young,
and dragons spoke the only tongue,
they ruled the lands and skies above,
and hoarded all the things they loved."

The heroes stopped what they were doing and all eyes fell on Witt.

Stu laughed. "This has to be the stupidest kobold I've ever met. He walks right into his death." Stu tossed the kobold he was holding to the side like she was a toy. "I can't wait to claim the reward for shutting him down." He lifted his warhammer off the ground and marched toward Witt.

Witt continued playing, keeping a safe distance between him and Stu.

"But then came men and dwarves and elves,
who wanted treasures for themselves.
The dragons retreated into the highest mountains,
where only the bravest heroes found them.
It was in this time kobolds were born,
to protect the dragons and their hoard.
They fought with axes, spears, and knives,
and made elaborate traps to hide."

As Inspired Frenzy took effect, the eyes of the restrained kobolds began to glow red. The heroes were so focused on him that only Witt saw what was happening around him. Every eye was focused on Stu and Witt's exchange. As the notes continued to find their way into the burrow, Witt knew there was a horde of kobolds with a festering rage underneath.

"They caught the heroes unaware..."

Witt snarled at Stu as the first kobold poked its head from the burrow.

"ambushed them in the dragon's lair.
The heroes wore resplendent armor,
carried rare weapons, cast spells with ardor.
But kobolds possessed the greater numbers,
and fought for all their sisters and brothers.
They ripped the armor from their bodies,
scalped their heads, for it was folly
to think that they could slay a dragon
when kobolds were the dragon's assassins."

The screams of dozens of kobolds tore through the night. Rage burned inside all of them, granting increased Strength, Dexterity, and Constitution. The citizens of Swampside attacked with a fervor powered by Witt's hatred for the heroes.

The kobolds restrained near the fire pit broke the ropes that bound them and swarmed the seven heroes. Kobolds poured from the burrows, outnumbering each hero a dozen to one.

Stu charged Witt, but he wasn't done yet. He strummed his lute again and it glowed white as he prepared Song of Silence.

Two kobolds lunged at Stu, grabbing him around the foot and slowing his charge. Stu smashed one with his hammer, but two more took its place.

"The world was dark and full of terror
for those who lived in the dragon era.
Blue, red, silver, and white,
no prey could hope to escape their might.
They burned castles and farms to the ground,

destroying families and razing towns.
And now the time has come again
for all to fear the dragon kin..."

Another massive strum sent the pent-up energy exploding across the village center like a flash of light. Stu's glowing warhammer faded mid-swing. A spell from the elven mage vanished just as she extended her hand to release. An empowered stomp by the minotaur did nothing more than stir up ash.

"What the hell have you done?" Stu snarled. "I'll kill you a thousand times over for this."

Kobolds ripped the armor from his shoulders and chest. Others pinned him to the ground and stabbed him, painting his tunic a vibrant red. Everywhere Witt looked it was the same. Dozens of kobolds lay dead, but they were overpowering the heroes by sheer force of will.

Two dwarves drew their last breaths, and the kobolds who killed them wasted no time joining their kin.

Witt was fueled by so much icy hatred that he was surprised he wasn't frozen to the ground.

One by one the heroes fell, until only Stu was left. He looked like a slaughtered boar as he lay on the ground, gasping for air. Pure, raw hatred poured from his eyes.

Witt smiled. He understood the feeling all too well.

He knelt down next to Stu, the dwarf responsible for setting him down his path. "It seems kobolds might not be as stupid as you first thought, huh?"

Stu growled, but Witt placed a cold finger to the dwarf's lips.

"Shhh. I'll do the talking. You just listen."

A vein in Stu's forehead threatened to explode.

"Before I get to the details, a thank you is in order. Because if not for you, I wouldn't be here right now. I wouldn't know of the countless murders bestowed upon us by your people." Witt shook his head. "No, I don't mean dwarves. I mean heroes. The common people will not be held responsible for your crimes." He leaned in closer until the chill of his breath cooled Stu's flushed cheeks. "Come for us again and you will receive far worse than what has happened to you today. Unlike Swampside, you will not find Murkwell unprepared." He removed his finger from Stu's lips. "Any last words?"

Stu opened his mouth, but before he had a chance to speak Witt pushed his dagger through the dwarf's throat.

Witt stood up and addressed the still-raging kobolds. "Carry what you can, leave behind the rest. You are all citizens of Murkwell now."

CHAPTER SIXTEEN

Witt led the displaced kobolds toward Murkwell. Their arms were full as they carried as much as they could to start their new lives. While the burrows of Swampside were still intact, the structures aboveground had been destroyed. Over half the population had been killed by the heroes, and another large portion had died during the final battle.

They simply didn't have the kobold power to rebuild. Even if they did rebuild, who would protect them? Who would keep Stu and his cronies from laying siege again and again?

If they came to Murkwell, Witt promised to take care of them. They were his people and they would always have a home wherever he was. His vision had grown bigger than protecting those who lived in his village; he wanted to change the world for kobolds all over.

He would do whatever it took to make that happen.

There were still notifications for Witt to sort through, but his mind was elsewhere. Stu wouldn't take this defeat lightly. He would come back for vengeance and probably bring more heroes with him next time. After killing seven more heroes, the bounty for shutting him down would be greater than ever.

They needed to be prepared. He hoped Zirn and the others had finished setting traps. Once he made it back to the village, he had a few more ideas to help with security.

Several of the stronger kobolds carried eggs from the Swampside hatchery. Their hatchery had fewer eggs than Murkwell, but there was no way they could leave them behind.

Witt wasn't sure what the plan was going forward. He'd never led a village before, but it was his actions that had gotten Swampside into this predicament. He needed to find a way to keep his people safe while fulfilling his quest at the same time.

The stronger he grew, the safer they would become. It was the intermediate part where they would face the most danger. He needed to level up fast.

As they walked in silence under the light of the moon, Witt pulled up his notifications.

––––––––

Notifications:

You have killed a level 10 hero. X2

You have killed a level 9 hero. X2

You have killed a level 11 hero.

You have killed a level 8 hero. X2

You have been awarded 7000 XP.

You have leveled up. You are now level 10.

You have leveled up. You are now level 11.

You have learned the ability Barbarian Rage (Barbarian).

Barbarian Rage: Gain increased Strength, Dexterity, and Constitution. While in a rage, user is unable to cast any non-barbarian abilities. After rage ends, user will suffer fatigue equal to the duration of the rage.

You have learned the ability Song of Seduction (Bard).

Song of Seduction: Ability to woo a neutral creature to your cause.

You have been awarded 175 Villain Points.

Quest Alert: *You have reached 300 Villain Points. Due to your notoriety, heroes will recognize you in passing. Guards of Skullheyden will also arrest you on sight. Other cities remain unaffected.*

Quest Alert: *You have reached 400 Villain Points. You are now eligible to lay claim to a town or village. If a town or village is unclaimed, you may lay claim. If a town or village has already been claimed, you may lay claim once it is no longer under another's domain.*

Quest Alert: *Due to your recent actions, you have also taken on the name The Unforgiving Kobold. For you, peace is not an option.*

That familiar cool crept over his shoulders. This was a big boon. With Barbarian Rage, he could finally buff himself without the lute. This would be great for fights, but he would lose access to all of his bard abilities until his rage was over. If he used it at the right time, it wouldn't matter.

Song of Seduction was an intriguing ability. Basically he could play a song and the animal or monster would fall under his influence. He wasn't much of a beastmaster or tamer, but perhaps an opportunity would present itself.

The real intrigue was his new quest alerts. Now that he had four hundred villain points, it was time to start thinking bigger. Kobold society had elders and powerful kobolds that were respected, but they didn't have leaders like humans and other races. There were no mayors or kings, not since Hugnu.

He had been the one and only kobold king. He'd risked everything for his people and in the end he'd still lost.

Witt had to be better.

Everything that the kobolds in Murkwell did benefitted the community. If Witt wanted to claim the village as his own and become a true villain, then he had to stake his authority.

He smiled at his new nickname, *The Unforgiving Kobold*. The notification was right. Peace was not an option, not anymore. He wouldn't stop until every hero knew to stay the hell away from Murkwell and its people.

The last thing he noticed was that his Strength and Charisma each had a stat point added automatically. He could feel the firmness of his muscles as they grew stronger. The added Charisma would certainly help with integrating the residents of Swampside into the village.

Witt wondered if he would sleep tonight. There was work to be done and plans to be made. Rest was a luxury for heroes.

They followed a narrow path through the forest. Only kobolds used it, so they could walk with room to spare. Most other races would have a hard time navigating the low-hanging branches and shrubbery.

Thanks to darkvision, the light of the moon was all that they needed to find their way. Witt buffed them with Song of Swiftness and soon they were on the border to Murkwell. Thick vegetation grew around the boundary, making it difficult to see inside the village. A small path led through a thicket, but it was undoubtedly full of traps.

Witt made the refugees wait behind him. He pulled out his lute and played the first few chords of Inspired Frenzy. The notes darted through the trees and bushes, letting Witt know that kobolds were nearby.

"It's Witt," he called into the darkness. "I've brought

kobolds from Swampside. They'll be staying with us now. Please disarm the traps so that we can enter."

A moment later a voice replied. "Give us a minute."

Several kobolds appeared on the path, disconnecting wires and loosening ropes.

"Come on in." One of the kobolds waved them forward. "Watch out for that spot." He pointed to a pile of dried leaves.

Witt wasn't sure who to talk to about sleeping arrangements for the new villagers. For as far back as he could remember, everyone just had their space.

If I want to be a great leader, then I need to start making the decisions. I can't wait around for someone to tell me what to do.

Witt found most of the village in the center around the fire pit. They were silent as he entered. For the first time in many moons, there was no laughter, no drinking, no raucous fights.

Their eyes followed him, each one waiting for answers.

Witt cleared his throat. He searched the group before him for friendly faces and found Kessy, Hux, Razul, and Zirn sitting next to one another. They'd taken to one another rather quickly and they would be his greatest source of insight going forward.

"Swampside is no more. The village was destroyed and many lives were lost. We managed to kill seven heroes, but at a great cost. They know who I am now, and it won't be long before they come looking. This is a trial we must survive. The remaining citizens of Swampside will be a part of our community going forward. They have brought what they could carry as well as the eggs from their hatchery. Make sure they find a safe place for them. I expect we will have many new young kobolds come morning."

Witt motioned for the refugees to join him. "Tomorrow, we start a new day in Murkwell. Kessy, I want you to make sure that our new brothers and sisters all find burrows. For the rest of you, no one is to leave the village tomorrow. Your days of mining and farming are over. I have plenty of work for you to do here. I suggest you all rest for the night. Hux, Zirn, Razul, I'd like to have a word with you."

Everyone disbanded and Witt took a seat around the fire.

"What happened?" asked Hux.

Witt leaned forward, hanging his head. His body threatened to crumple, the tension inside too much to bear. He was finally safe at home and a wave of emotion threatened to drown him. "This was all my fault. They all died because of me."

Razul shook his head. "No, they died because of the heroes. They made the choice to attack the village. The same way they made the choice to kill us over and over for sport."

Zirn put a hand on Witt's arm. "You can't blame yourself for this. You are a gift. For once, we have a chance to be great again. To be respected. You can't let one setback deter you from what must be done."

He sighed again. They were right. He couldn't let the devastation he witnessed hinder him from what needed to be done.

The kobold in the corner of his vision pulsed, signaling he had a new notification. He quickly pulled it up.

Notifications:

Quest Alert: *You have entered the village of Murkwell. It currently remains unclaimed. Would you like to claim Murkwell, making it your stronghold?*

Witt nodded, accepting the prompt, and another notification appeared.

Quest Alert: Congratulations! You have claimed the village of Murkwell as your stronghold. It will remain under your control until your villain points reach zero or the village is usurped by another. Note: only those with titles may claim strongholds.

The ground rumbled and a second later, a wave of energy expanded across the village. The trees swished and several animals bolted in alarm. Then the village sat in silence aside from the crackle of the fire.

The other three kobolds looked at Witt with confounded expressions.

"Most interesting." Hux's expression changed from one of confusion to mischief. "It has been many years since a kobold laid claim to a stronghold."

Witt stood up, pacing back and forth in front of the fire. "Tomorrow, we will begin plans to turn Murkwell into a fortress. Put all of the miners and farmers to work. I want a palisade around the perimeter. I want guards posted at every tunnel leading in and out of the village at all times."

Zirn nodded. "We'll get to it first thing in the morning."

"Good. Then tomorrow night, we go hunting."

CHAPTER SEVENTEEN

Witt worked through the night while the rest of Murkwell slumbered. Scouts still watched the trapped entrances but aside from them, the village was empty. Eerily empty. Even Olah's boar kept his snorts to himself.

Usually, there were at least a few drunken revelers partying well past bedtime. Schekt was among them more often than not.

Witt took one of the hidden tunnels, bypassing the traps, and emerged outside of the village and into the dense forest. He snuck as quietly as he could, making notes that would be helpful the next night.

By the break of dawn, Witt had circled the entire perimeter of the village and found himself back at the hidden tunnel. He felt confident in his recon. His eyes were blood-shot and scratchy, but he stuck to his motto. *No rest for the wicked.*

The village center was crowded when Witt arrived. The addition of the kobolds from Swampside made them a formidable force. Gerah, one of the nurse mothers from the hatchery, approached Witt.

"We've had nearly two dozen eggs hatch overnight. Many more are shaking, and it looks like they will be hatching in the coming days." She beamed with pride.

"Excellent." Witt returned her smile. "Make sure you have everything you need. Ask Kessy, and she will see that it is done."

The time had come for Witt to start delegating. For once, he had more on his plate than he could handle. The new addition of the young kobolds would help replenish their ranks, but it took months for them to mature into productive members of society. Months that Witt wasn't sure they had.

He took his familiar place on top of the boulder and addressed the crowd. "Today is the beginning of a new era for kobolds. One where we no longer suffer disrespect and contempt with a smile. One where we take what is ours." Witt scanned the crowd and his eyes rested on Kessy. She smiled and nodded. "You may be wondering what that is. For now, it is Murkwell. This is our home, and our fortress. We have drifted under everyone's noses for too long. Only noticed when we had a part to play or if they thought we were in the way." Witt paused, and his lip curled into a snarl. "But they are noticing us now. And they will forever remember what happens when you wake a sleeping dragon!"

The crowd hissed and roared in response. They would fight and die for him if he asked. They would leap into the Pit of Despair at his command. Witt had his army, he had his power, now he needed to learn how to wield it.

He held his hand in the air and waited for them to quiet. "Farmers, I want you with Zirn. Today we will be putting that famous kobold work ethic to good use. I want a palisade surrounding the village by nightfall. Miners, today you will trade your pickaxe for a saw. We need lumber to build our defenses. Clear the perimeter surrounding the village, it will aid us in spotting our attackers and provide the materials we need for our safety. Today will be tough, but it will be worth it. The rest of you, make sure we are well stocked on food and supplies. We need spears and arrows. This may be your last day to enter the city, so empty the coffers and buy what you can. Zirn, Hux, Kessy, and Razul, I'd like a word."

His four most trusted allies joined him at the foot of the boulder.

"You look tired. Did you sleep at all last night?" Hux squinted as he looked Witt over.

"I'll sleep when I'm dead." Witt laughed. "Zirn, I want you in charge of building the palisade. Feel free to add any tricks and traps you have at your disposal. Move the ones you have further out. I want these heroes hurt and bleeding long before they ever make it to the walls."

"I'll see that it is done." Zirn turned to the group. "Farmers, you're with me. Let's get moving."

"Razul, Hux, I want you in charge of lumber and clearing the area around the village. I want scorched earth between the forest and the new palisade. Any hero that emerges from the forest will be an easy target as they charge the wall."

The two nodded, and then gathered the miners.

"Kessy, you're the only one of us who can set foot in Skullheyden at the moment. Take the wagons and the others and go buy as much as you can. I don't fear Skullheyden will attack us, but we need to be prepared for a siege."

Kessy moved in closer and placed a hand on Witt's arm. "I'm proud of you, Witt. However this all ends, I'll be by your side through it all."

He placed his hand on top of hers and a warmth traveled up his fingers. "You always have been my biggest supporter. Thanks for believing in me."

While Kessy went to fetch supplies with the others, Witt set to empowering his people. Zirn and the farmers removed the traps they had painstakingly engineered the day before, and the miners went to work chopping trees and clearing brush from the village borders.

The task was simple enough that Witt could use his influence over the kobolds to somewhat control them while playing Inspired Frenzy. The raging miners hacked and sawed with increased vigor. Occasionally, a fight would break out as two miners competed to see who could saw a tree faster. Razul would break them up and after a cool-down period they would be back to work again.

With every foot of cleared forest, Hux erupted a wall of flame, cleansing the earth of shrubbery and debris. Song of Enlightenment kept his mana regenerated so that he could keep up with the demand. Soon, they were running like a well-oiled machine and clearing the forest in droves.

Once the traps were reset deeper into the forest, the farmers set to erecting a palisade from the downed trees. The tops of the trees that would make up the wall were carved into spikes. The excess branches were set aside to be used as spears and arrows. With the help of the tinkerers, they used a system of ropes and pulleys to move the stakes into position, arranging them one beside the other with no space in between. It would be a sturdy defense, and kobolds could still bombard anyone on the other side by climbing the trees inside the village walls.

Kobolds moved like ants with everyone constantly working. Witt's voice ached from the constant singing. His head pounded and his vision blurred at objects in the distance. Even on his busiest days at the dungeon, he had never buffed so much. By noon, he was thoroughly exhausted.

"Here, take this." Razul handed him a vial of green liquid.

Witt examined it.

Item. Greater Stamina Potion. *Restores stamina completely.*

He downed the green liquid. It was surprisingly sweet and

syrupy. So much so that he thought he might gag as it slowly descended down his throat.

Once he got over the discomfort, a sudden relief coursed through his body. The pounding headache faded along with the sore throat, and his vision was crisp and clear once again.

"Wow, thanks. Where'd that come from?"

Razul winked. "I stole it from the caravan before we trashed them. I figured today was as good a day as any to use it. Time is of the essence after all."

That was the truth of it. After a quick break for lunch they were all back to work.

By early afternoon the exterior of the village was unrecognizable. Nearly half of the palisade had been erected and three quarters of the perimeter had been cleared. Murkwell was beginning to look like a formidable town and less like a hidden village. Normally, this rate of production would have been impossible, but thanks to Witt they were moving at an astounding pace.

For the next few hours, he continued to buff his people as they fortified Murkwell with anger and rage. As the sun began to wane, Witt spotted Kessy and Olah with a train of people coming to the main entrance. The wagons were loaded with supplies, so much so that they shook with every bump on the trail. The stragglers carried baskets full of potions, meat, vegetables, and other items.

"We spent it all. Every last coin the village had." Kessy beamed with pride. She paused for a moment to look at her surroundings. "I can't believe you did this in a day. It's barely recognizable."

Witt grinned. "Never underestimate the power of a group of raging kobolds. Go ahead and make sure everything is stored safely underground, you can fill me in on what you picked up over dinner. We still have work to do out here."

The village continued working past twilight. The palisade

was ninety percent complete, and Witt was faced with a decision. Should he press on with construction or go ahead with
his plan to level up? Perhaps he could have both.

A defensive structure was important, but he needed his
people stronger if they hoped to survive what was coming.

"Dig in!" Witt moved aside and waited for everyone to
grab their food before taking his own.

Several cheers resounded as they carved the suckling hog
from the spit. As they ate, chatter was minimal and no one
drank kobold brew. There would be a time for celebration,
but it wasn't tonight. There was still work to do and they all
knew it. Even Schekt sat in silence as he ate.

Witt's council joined him.

Zirn spoke first. "I'm amazed by the progress we made
today. Once the wall is finished, I pity anyone who dares set
foot in Murkwell uninvited."

"Hear, hear!" Razul lifted a dagger that pierced through a
slab of meat. "What's the plan for tonight, boss?"

"We'll get to that. First, I want to know about our new
supplies."

Kessy wiped her mouth on her tunic. "Where to begin? I
bought potions. I don't know much about them, but heroes
use them after battle, so I thought they might be a good idea.
We got elixirs, boom powder, an assortment of weapons,
armor, enough food to last us for a few weeks even if we can't
go out to hunt. And I got this for you." She reached in the
pouch hanging from her side and pulled out a necklace with a
green stone in the pendant.

"What is this?" Witt took the pendant and felt a surge of
energy rush through his body.

"It's an amulet. It is supposed to offer you protection."

Witt analyzed the amulet.

Item. *Jade Amulet.* +3 *Charisma to bards.* *This mystical* *stone is said to bring good fortune to the wearer, and ward off evil spirits.*

Witt placed the amulet around his neck. The green stone seemed to have an energy of its own inside it. "Thank you, Kessy. I'm sure this will be of great use someday."

Kessy flushed and her eyes darted into the forest.

Witt pressed his fingers to the stone. This was an item designed for heroes; he'd seen many like it in the market on his way to the dungeon each day. And yet here he was, soon to use their own items against them.

He finished his meat and stood up. It was time to get back to work. He strummed his lute to gather everyone's attention.

"Farmers, it is time to finish the palisade. I will buff you one final time before we head out. Tomorrow, you all will join the hunt. Everyone else, gather your weapons. Spears are best if you have them, but anything will do, even a pickaxe. Once you are ready, meet me at the gate."

The farmers got to work. Directed by the tinkerers and buffed by Inspired Frenzy, they moved logs with fervor. Witt had no doubt they would be finished by the time he returned.

A crowd awaited Witt when he returned to the gate. They were much more prepared than the times he had sent them in a rage to fight the troll. This time, they were heavily armed. He would make sure no one died tonight.

Witt pulled a piece of parchment out of his pouch and held it up in the air. "Last night, I scouted beyond our borders and made a list of all the monsters that resided here. While they roam freely during the day, most of them return to the same place at night to sleep. If by some chance they have been killed during the day, then they will respawn in the same area come morning. Tonight, we are going to clear the forest and all of you will grow stronger." He tucked the parchment away. "Silence is of the utmost importance, therefore I will not be buffing you for this. We will attack quietly and in unison, and you will all see the morning."

Witt found it strange that he suddenly cared so much whether his fellow kobolds lived or died. Death had never meant much to him before. All kobolds were reborn in the hatchery and their spirit lived on. But now, when he lost a kobold, he was losing their utility. It would take months for a hatchling to replace them. He didn't value their lives for their spirit and personality. He valued them for what they could do for him.

Perhaps he was a villain.

"First stop, the troll."

A single tinkerer traveled with them to spot traps and disarm them when needed. The group walked through the forest like silent assassins; the only sounds were the snapping of an occasional twig or the hoot of an owl in the distance.

They came upon the familiar sight of the boil-covered troll as it slept raucously through the night.

Kobolds surrounded the troll on every side, swords drawn and spears raised. More climbed into the trees with their bows and arrows.

Witt lifted his hand and curled it into a fist. When he lowered it, the troll barely had time to groan before the life faded from its eyes.

One down, a whole forest to go.

After killing a family of bears, satyrs, an ogre, and a group of monstrous shrubs, some of the level-one kobolds had leveled up. Witt quickly realized that this wouldn't be as easy or as quick as he thought. The group was too big and the experience too few to level them all like this. He would need to take them in smaller groups if he hoped to make a real dent. The best fighters and those with the most to gain would be the priority. They needed strong fighters that could go head to head with the heroes even though they didn't have abilities.

Witt needed to think.

"That's it for tonight. I'm sure you can all use the rest. We'll get back at this tomorrow."

Hux stepped next to Witt. "Is everything okay? There is still plenty of night left."

Witt clenched his fist, angry that he hadn't thought of the division of experience points. Up until now, all of the experience had gone to him and him alone. No wonder he had leveled up so fast. "This isn't going to work. It's too slow. I need a faster way to level them up. Let's get back to the village."

"You heard the skald," Razul shouted. "Back to the village."

"It wasn't a bad plan." Kessy tried to comfort him. "Sometimes things just don't work out the way we imagine."

"I don't have time to fail." Witt shook his head in desperation. "There is a target on my back and if I lose, we all lose."

Snapping branches echoed from deep in the forest. There was an explosion of light, and then more branches snapped.

Witt grew cold all over. Was it the heroes? Had they regrouped so quickly?

"Everyone back to the village!" Witt shouted, but he didn't run. He would face whatever abomination was coming. With a dagger in each hand, it was time to fight.

The patter of kobold feet rolled like a gentle breeze behind them while a tidal wave of doom threatened to swallow him from the front.

Witt would hold them off as long as he could to give his people a chance at safety.

A shadowy figure appeared to his right, and then Hux joined his left.

"You two need to run. If you die, you won't respawn."

Witt appreciated the gesture, but he couldn't afford to lose them. If he died, he'd wake up back in the village.

Razul twirled a dagger around his finger. "Then I guess we better not die then. How's that sound to you, Hux?"

Hux gripped his staff. "You know, I have grown quite fond of living."

Witt couldn't help but smile. He could probably use his influence to make them leave, but he knew he would catch hell for it. If they wanted to fight by his side, who was he to stop them?

"Alright. No one dies. Except for whoever is tearing the forest to pieces."

There was another flare of light and then a loud scream. They could see the trees shaking in the darkness. Whatever was coming, it was almost there.

"Help me! Somebody, anybody, help!" A kobold wearing bright-yellow robes ripped and covered in mud jumped through the bushes. He tripped on a root and fell to the ground.

Wide-eyed and full of panic, he clawed to his feet. "Run! The wolf spiders, they've chased me all the way from the mountain!"

The kobold turned and lifted a golden scepter the length of his forearm, pointing it toward the shaking trees. Light flared out from the end of the scepter in a golden arc, blinding Witt and momentarily stopping the rustling leaves.

"Come on, we can take haven in Murkwell." The robed kobold scrambled to his feet.

The stars faded from Witt's vision and he exchanged glances with Razul and Hux. "How many are there?"

The robed kobold scrunched his eyes. "Four, now let's go."

Witt shook his head. "No, we stay and fight."

No sooner had he finished his words than the first wolf spider emerged from the bushes. Long hairy legs tipped with claws dug into the earth. Pincers snapped viciously, and an angry set of milky yellow eyes scanned the forest.

The group instinctively took a step back. Hux cast a flame wall just as two other spiders joined their brother. The spiders hissed violently from behind the flames.

"Do you have a death wish?" asked the kobold in yellow.

"We can talk later, for now, we fight." Witt readied his daggers.

Hux tossed a fireball that passed through the flame wall, hitting one of the spiders in the face. It shrieked in pain as hair melted from its face.

The flame wall faded and all hell broke loose.

Witt activated Scale Mail and Critical Strike. Thanks to his recent levels, he was faster and stronger than ever.

The spiders lunged at the four kobolds. Witt ducked and slid underneath the spider's belly, dragging his daggers across the soft underside as he slid. The bottom of the abdomen ripped open, spilling a slimy green substance.

Hux pummeled fireballs and attacked with his staff, while Razul put all of his rogue sneakery to use, moving in and out of the shadows and delivering critical strike after critical strike.

One of the spiders launched a glob of acid. It shot by Hux, melting foliage before sizzling out on the forest floor.

The new kobold wielded his scepter with grace, shooting beams of light that burned, slowed, and dissipated into the spiders. It was a spectacle to behold.

A clawed foot ripped through Witt's tunic, but the buff from Scale Mail mitigated most of the damage.

Witt watched as an orb of light traveled through the spider's body. It looked as if the spell had failed, then light burst through its black abdomen. At first, it was just a pinprick of light, as if a balloon were leaking. Light shot through, at first only a trickle and then more and more holes appeared until the light erupted like the quills of a porcupine. The spider's insides sizzled and then the abdomen exploded, raining innards upon them all.

Razul managed to stake one of the spider's claws into a tree stump as Hux summoned a flame wall underneath the beast, burning it alive.

The final two spiders were easy prey to the four kobolds.

Witt activated Barbarian Rage and felt a power inside him unlike anything he had ever experienced. Hot rage flowed through him, empowering his muscles with strength and adrenaline. His insides ached with unspent energy waiting to be released.

He leapt into the air, spinning and twisting so that he landed on the back of a spider. Flames engulfed the spider beside him, but Witt paid it no mind. He stabbed violently as energy from Cleave shot out in waves. Green blood spurted from each new wound as the spider thrashed beneath him.

A beam of light hit the spider in the face, stunning it. Witt used the opportunity to stab all eight eyes, blinding the furry arachnid. It screeched in pain, leaving a ringing in Witt's ears, but it was too late. The spider stumbled back and forth as blood loss overtook it.

With a final sigh, the spider collapsed. As Witt's rage faded, his muscles ached, the post-rage fatigue setting in.

He sat down and wiped spider guts from his face with his tunic. Then he turned to the new kobold. "Who are you and where did you come from?"

Although he looked similar to every other kobold, brilliant golden eyes set him apart. "I'm Mido, the light mage from Swampside. I was a part of a quest in Corvin Mountain when a dragon took over the dungeon. Apparently it flew all the way from New Hope Cove. Everyone was in hysterics. The heroes inside the dungeon were all burned alive. I managed to sneak out through a secret exit and made my way down Machmuller Pass, only to find it overrun with wolf spiders. The ones we just killed followed me all the way down the mountain."

"Wait, did you say dragon? There's a dragon in the mountain?" Witt's heart raced. He'd always dreamed of seeing a dragon. "What was it like?"

Mido smiled. "The most terrifyingly beautiful thing you will ever witness. Scales the color of pure gold. Fire that can melt rock. Power and grace that leaves you in awe just by laying eyes on it. No wonder the heroes died. No one remains stoic in the face of a dragon."

"I'm afraid I have some bad news." Witt frowned. "Swampside is no more."

Mido scrunched his eyes in confusion. "What do you mean?"

Witt told him of the attack and the heroes and everything that had happened the past few days. "We could use your help in Murkwell."

Mido clasped his hands together. "If Murkwell is where my people are, then I will defend them until the end." He extended a hand and Witt clasped him around the wrist.

Another mage joins my cause. We may survive this yet.

CHAPTER EIGHTEEN

Hundreds of kobolds were waiting at the gate when Witt arrived. They held spears, swords, and bows at the ready. Several more hid in the trees with ranged weapons.

Witt smiled. They had retreated, but they hadn't given up.

He waved them all to calm down. "It's okay. They were wolf spiders from Corvin Mountain. Since Hux hasn't been to his post in a couple of days, they've overtaken the pass. You can all rest now. Tomorrow we will start training."

Most kobolds were natural fighters to a degree, but Razul agreed to show them some basic moves that should help their chances at survival.

Zirn waited around after the crowd had begun to fade. He looked tired, but wore a smile. "The palisade is completed. We can all sleep easy tonight."

Witt clasped him on the shoulder. "Thank you for making this happen."

"We couldn't have done it without your buffs. Without your leadership."

Witt simply nodded. He didn't consider himself a great leader, but he had managed to erect a wall and traps around

Murkwell in under a day. He had united two villages and brought them to his cause.

He introduced Mido to the others. "He says there is a dragon in Corvin Mountain. It flew all the way up from New Hope Cove."

Just as Witt expected, their mouths hung open in shock.

Kessy bounced on the balls of her feet. "This can't be a coincidence. First you get your quest, and now this. We descended from dragons, you know."

Witt laughed at her enthusiasm, though he wasn't sure it was warranted. "I know. The blood of the dragons flows through us all. I'm not a dragon rider, though. Nothing is calling me toward the mountain. We can be grateful that many heroes will likely die trying to best the dungeon. That is a victory in itself. It's been a long day, though. I suggest we all get some sleep."

The walls of the burrow shook, jostling Witt awake. Pieces of dirt and rock rained down from the ceiling, resting on his head and shoulders.

Something was wrong. He could feel it in his bones. Witt's heart raced as he grabbed his lute and daggers before rushing out of the tunnel.

Other kobolds were already running toward the surface. The walls stopped shaking momentarily, and he spotted Kessy up ahead.

"Kessy, what's going on?" He hurried to her side.

Her eyes were wide as she looked around. "I don't know."

The earth quaked again just as they made it aboveground. A massive boulder had erupted from the earth, splintering the newly built palisade by the gate. Early-morning sunlight bathed the village; it would have been beautiful if not for the chaos unfolding.

Witt cursed under his breath. He knew who was responsible. One of the other dwarves in Stu's party was an earth mage. The ground continued to shake as a second boulder emerged, uprooting the stakes that Zirn and the others had so painstakingly assembled.

All that hard work, gone in an instant. It was a somber reminder of just how powerful heroes truly were. One mage could singlehandedly dismantle their defenses. Why had they not founded Murkwell inside of a mountain?

All around him, kobolds rushed to and fro gathering weapons and taking positions. Witt stood there motionless. Useless.

He didn't understand how this was possible. How had they made it past the traps, especially during the night?

The gate rumbled as something on the other side pounded it repeatedly.

Witt needed to get moving, but he was at a loss for where to begin. A glass orb shot over the wall and exploded into flames when it hit the ground. Several more followed, setting the village ablaze. Horses neighed as flames coated the stables.

Kobolds climbed into the trees near the perimeter, firing arrows at the intruders.

Zirn bumped into Witt as he exited the tunnel pushing a wagon full of vials filled with liquids and powders of various colors. "Do something, Witt!"

Weaponless kobolds flocked to the wagon, grabbing vials and running toward the palisade.

Screams assaulted his ears as shards of ice shot over the wall, impaling kobolds who had taken position in the trees.

With a crash, the gate cracked down the middle and a steaming orc stepped through. Heat radiated from his skin.

He lifted his battleaxe in the air, and tilted his head back, roaring as more heroes rushed past.

More than a dozen heroes spilled through the gate. Witt's blood turned to ice when he spotted Stu leading the assault, his warhammer raised high in the air.

Kobolds charged at the intruders, but a blue-clad gnome raised her arms and the ground before her turned to ice. The kobolds slipped and fell, sliding right into the attacks of the heroes.

Witt watched helplessly as Stu crushed the skull of a kobold with his hammer. The barbarian orc stomped another. Everywhere he looked, it was the same. Devastation.

His hatred for Stu took over. He slung his lute over his shoulder and grabbed his daggers. He'd go into a rage and he would kill him. He'd kill him again and again until the end of time.

As if sensing his train of thought, Kessy grabbed Witt by the arm. "This is bigger than him."

Witt jerked his arm free. He turned to Kessy, ready to lash out. She didn't understand what he had been through, what he had experienced.

The concern in her eyes told him otherwise. Witt wasn't special in his suffering. He was just in a position to finally do something about it.

Kessy was right. This wasn't about one particular hero. This was about all heroes. Stu hadn't been the only one to kill him. Stu wasn't the only hero tearing down Murkwell's walls. They were all the problem.

Witt put his daggers away and pulled out his lute. He strummed the chords and began singing.

"In ancient times, when lands were young,
and dragons spoke the only tongue,
they ruled the lands and skies above,
and hoarded all the things they loved..."

"Hey!" Kessy called to the kobolds near her. "We protect Witt at all costs!"

A circle of kobolds with glowing red eyes surrounded Witt as he belted the lines of Inspired Frenzy. Musical notes darted from his lute, empowering kobolds with skaldic power. All around him, kobolds began to rage. A mob of them swarmed the dwarven paladin, ripping his armor off as he exploded with holy light.

The mob suddenly stopped attacking as an aura of pink energy surrounded them. Their tongues draped from their mouths like limp noodles, the rage all but gone.

A burly, shirtless human approached them. He walked calmly, with no urgency whatsoever. His chest hair was shaved into the shape of a heart and a massive beard framed his jawline. He blew a kiss at one of the kobolds, and a pink heart made of energy zoomed toward the kobold. It dissipated into the kobold's body and his raging eyes turned to hearts. He walked to the man where he was promptly choked to death.

As Witt finished Inspired Frenzy, kobolds fought against heroes nearly ten to one, but they were losing. The magical abilities of the heroes were too much.

Hux battled with the ice mage, their spells nullifying one another and covering the area in steam. Zirn peppered the group of heroes with throwables as they pushed their way deeper into the village. Razul was nowhere to be seen, but Witt was certain he was wreaking havoc somewhere.

I need to silence them. It was the only way to even the playing field.

The orc slashed his axe in an arc, dropping half a dozen kobolds with a single attack. A vial of boom powder exploded against his chest, turning his green skin bright red and knocking him to the ground. More kobolds flocked to the downed orc.

Stu tossed his warhammer. It cracked the skull of a nearby kobold, killing it instantly, before returning to the warrior's hand.

"Joaquin, see if you can spot the bard," Stu ordered.

From the backline of the heroes, a gnome wearing tight-fitting clothing hovered in the air. He held his hands firmly by his side and rose higher into the air, circled by a murder of crows. Kobolds shot arrows at the gnome, but the crows dove in front of the arrows, knocking them aside.

"There!" the gnome shouted. "They are protecting something in the back. They've formed a circle around a kobold playing an instrument."

Witt continued to play.

"The world was dark and full of terror
for those who lived in the dragon era.
Blue, red, silver, and white,
no prey could hope to escape their might.
They burned castles and farms to the ground..."

His lute glowed white as it built up energy. In the chaos that unfolded two scenes played out. A horde of kobolds fought desperately and without fear against the heroes that continued to press toward Witt. Then there was the force that protected Witt, an unmoving wall that would hold until their dying breath.

Kessy headed the second.

Witt finished Song of Silence and a wave of energy flared around him. Spells faltered mid-casting and the kobolds turned the tide. Heroes retreated as they attempted to cast spells to no effect.

Witt almost lost focus when he spotted Schekt, eyes glowing red, holding a sword over his shoulder and charging into the front lines.

"Greetings, adventurer!" Schekt roared. "Welcome to The Merry Minotaur!" He stabbed the hero in the neck, and blood spurted out in an arc. "Would you like a room or a drink?"

A dark shadow appeared in the center of the heroes as Razul stabbed an elf through the eye, killing it instantly.

The victory was short lived, as the barbarian orc grabbed Razul by the throat. The orc lifted him in the air as the rogue's eyes bulged from his reptilian face.

A blast of golden light collided with the orc and Razul dropped to the ground. Mido stood atop a boulder in a fighting stance, his wand pointed at the orc.

As the heroes realized they had been silenced, the warriors and damage dealers took the front lines, bashing kobolds with violent fury.

It was only a matter of time before they were on Witt. They would kill every last kobold to get to him. Despair started to creep in until his throat was thick and he had to fight for each breath. The world sped up and slowed down as everything dipped in and out of focus.

Witt stopped playing. It was clear they couldn't win this fight. The walls had been broken, his people killed, if he didn't do something soon, there would be no one left.

"Zirn!" Witt shouted. He pushed his way through the kobolds defending him. "Zirn!"

The kobold sea parted as Witt found the tinkerer tossing throwables from his wagon.

"I'm a little busy at the moment, Witt." Zirn continued to launch vial after vial.

"I need you to ready the Kobold Cannon."

Zirn froze mid throw. "Witt, now is not the time for games."

"It's not a game. This is the only way to save Murkwell. If I go, the village can be rebuilt, but if I stay they will burn it to the ground along with every kobold in it. The heroes will come for me."

Zirn paused for a moment, watching his village fall around him. "Fine, but we must hurry."

Several kobolds sat atop the cannon, using it as a perch to rain arrows on the heroes.

"Down!" Zirn yelled as he climbed up the cannon.

He adjusted the trajectory and cranked the lever as the bow pulled back into position. Witt climbed into the seat and felt the wood press against his back. His heart pounded.

"Ready?" asked Zirn.

"Ready."

There was a click as the lever flipped and the cannon propelled him through the air. He soared over the heroes and past the palisade. As he flew through the air like a dragon, Witt spotted Kessy down below.

"Find me in the mountain!" he yelled as the first tree limb smacked him in the face.

CHAPTER NINETEEN

Branches scraped against Witt's face and shoulders as he catapulted through the treetops toward the ground. Scale Mail kept the pain to a minimum, fortifying his scales with enough damage reduction to prevent the branches from tearing his skin. The pine trees were more forgiving than the oak, bending instead of breaking. When he collided with an oak limb thicker than he was, Witt found himself falling to the earth and gasping for breath.

The forest floor finished the job the limb had started. Witt croaked for air as he clawed at the earth.

He'd managed to escape the heroes, but it would only be a matter of time before they came looking for him. He hoped no more kobolds died in the process, though he had seen many fall even as he soared above the village. They'd lost too many already.

His notifications flashed, telling him that he had received seventy-five villain points for the three heroes who had died. He quickly pushed it away. They'd lost the battle, and if he didn't get moving, they would certainly lose the war.

Breath slowly returned, allowing Witt to focus. There was only one place he would be safe from the heroes. One place where he could hide and formulate a new plan. If the dragon had overtaken Corvin Mountain, that's the last place they would look for him.

Witt removed the twigs and leaves that had lodged in his lute. He played Song of Swiftness, and his legs moved in a blur as he bolted through the forest.

He passed the nearby forest troll and a moment later a boulder smashed into a tree. The troll pursued him for a moment before returning to its clearing.

He found the trail that led to the main road and followed it. The road from Skullheyden to Corvin Mountain was sparsely populated. With no kobolds going to work or heroes tackling the dungeon, only those bringing supplies up and down the mountain were about.

Regardless, Witt pulled his hood up, concealing his face. There could still be heroes heading to the pass. With Song of Swiftness buffing him, he passed by travelers before they ever had a chance to get a good look at him.

At Machmuller Pass, a group of gnomes ran in fear, chased by a pack of wolf spiders.

Witt smirked. Just one of the many ways that unappreciated kobolds added to society.

"It's not worth it! It's not worth it!" a gnome screamed.

"We were just trying to sell our goods across the mountain!" A second gnome tossed a trinket over his shoulder, but the spiders kept chasing.

Witt let them be. He had bigger problems to deal with at the moment.

The first thing he noticed as he made his way up the mountain was the gaping hole near the top of Corvin Mountain. The stone was smooth and glimmering in the sun, polished to perfection under fiery dragon breath. The surrounding trees and foliage were charred beyond saving. The dragon had literally melted its way through the mountain to take refuge.

A chill ran down Witt's spine. *To have that kind of power.*

He clenched his fist. He might not have the power of a dragon, but he had its desire. He had the blood of its ancestors in his veins. The heroes would suffer soon enough. He just needed time to think and plan. The fear of the dragon would give him just that.

Witt bypassed the mines, and made his way further up the mountain. He'd never been to The Cursed Catacombs. The entrance was underwhelming, in spite of it being a higher-level dungeon, offering tougher opponents and greater loot than The Forgotten Quarters Dungeon. The entrance was nothing more than a small cave. It could have passed for a mine entrance if not for the wooden sign engraved with the dungeon's name.

A scroll had been nailed over the sign. "Warning! Dragon inside. Certain death and dismemberment await anyone under level fifty who dares to enter."

Level fifty! Just how powerful was this dragon?

Witt laughed to himself. A dragon commanded respect just by existing. If Witt wanted to be a truly great villain, then he needed that same kind of respect. More than that, he needed to be feared.

The fact that he had been attacked by so many heroes was proof that they thought he was an easy target. He sighed. Some things never changed.

Inside, the cave transformed into a tunnel which led to a majestic hall. Torches lined the walls of the dungeon. In spite of the lackluster appearance on the outside, the interior was magnificent. Stone columns, intricately carved, held up a ceiling painted with beautiful depictions of orcs battling monsters.

Witt knew the history of The Cursed Catacombs. Long before Skullheyden had risen to prominence, Corvin Mountain had been temporarily ruled by orcs. The orc chieftain, wanting to command the respect of the other races, declared himself king and forced goblins to mine a stronghold within the mountain. To display his power, he laid claim to the tallest mountain in the area.

But orcs were not meant to live in mountains. Unrest quickly spread among the citizens and a mutiny formed. The mutineers believed that orcs should not stoop to the level of humans and dwarves. Orcs ruled the forest and were one with the beasts within. They took advice from their chieftain, but were not his slaves.

Having a king defied all of that.

One night, a battle raged within the throne room, and when a berserker destroyed a column, the ceiling caved in, killing all those inside.

Witt knew more lore than he could ever hope to use. As a skald, his knowledge of history was what fueled his songs. Each song told a story. And if he ever found himself with a spell designed for orcs, perhaps The Cursed Catacombs would come into play.

"Young one..." a snakelike voice called.

Witt jumped at the sudden noise. He looked over his shoulder but there was no one there. The hallway was empty except for the crackling torches.

"No one is there, young one. All flee under my gaze... Or they suffer the flames."

Witt pressed his back to the wall and armed himself with his daggers. Was it possible some hero still hid in the dungeon? His eyes darted from corner to corner, and inspecting the shadows of the columns.

"Of course. The young ones do not remember the ancient ways. They do not remember the call."

"Who's there?" Witt's voice cracked.

He pointed his daggers into the room, but no one revealed themselves.

"Do not address me in the common tongue!" The walls of the dungeon shook. *"Are you not the spawn of dragons?"*

It was then that Witt realized that the voice was speaking to him in draconic. He knew the language, all kobolds did, but it wasn't spoken often, not even in Murkwell.

"Who are you?" Witt asked in Draconic.

"Do you not know? Do you not feel my presence all around you?"

The icy patch on the back of his neck spread, creeping into his brain and down his spine.

"Are you the dragon?" The words were barely a whisper.

The voice laughed. *"There we go. Some of our intelligence still resides in you yet. Many know me as Vang the Undying, though my true name has not been spoken in ages. Now, come to me, I wish to look upon your face."*

Witt shivered. Vang the Undying, the only dragon that he knew still existed, had just requested his presence. Most kobolds would kill for this opportunity. Maybe he could use this to his advantage.

"Are you speaking through my mind?" The words of the dragon didn't sound like they were coming from one particular direction, but from everywhere.

"The connection between dragons and kobolds has existed since the days the first dragons pulled your lot from the fires. Have you not felt it burning within you? In your blood and bones?"

Witt froze. He had always known there was something there, something dying to break free. Many in Murkwell spoke of the dragon's fire during nights of revelry.

"How do I find you?" He couldn't explain it, but he

needed to see the dragon, to lay his eyes on the most fearsome creature in existence. He needed inspiration.

The dungeon trembled and a moment later a gust of hot air washed over Witt.

"Follow the heat."

Witt followed the hot air as a battle of fire and ice raged inside of him. The fire called to him from his very being, but the ice within him refused to melt. Was it possible to have both the cold cunning and the fiery rage?

The empty dungeon echoed with his every step. Even the monsters that protected the halls had fled from the dragon's presence. Nothing but a hero was foolish enough to challenge such power.

He passed empty room after empty room as the air grew warmer. Up stairs and down hallways. When it was so hot that even he felt uncomfortable, Witt knew he was close. Rubble littered the hallway that led to the throne room.

It had been built in the heart of the mountain, far away from those who might attack. But dragons had no bounds. Not even the mountain could stop them from taking what was theirs.

Witt stepped into the throne room and a gust of hot air pushed him back. The open roof revealed blue skies overhead, and curled atop the rubble a golden dragon blew smoke from its nose.

If not for the penetrating red eyes that followed Witt as he entered the room, Vang could have been a statue. Its golden scales gleamed in the sunlight. Whether from the natural sheen or the heat that resided inside the monster, the air shimmered around it. The massive creature was bigger than any beast Witt had ever seen in the forest. If the gods were real, then they were certainly dragons.

Vang rose up, stretching its back and sending rubble scattering. Witt instinctively knelt before his ancestor.

"You are wise beyond your years." Vang lifted its head, red eyes piercing into Witt. *"What is it that brings a young one like yourself to my domain?"*

"Safety," Witt croaked. "We are being hunted and killed, all because I have power."

Vang laughed and flames poured from its throat. *"What power do you have?"*

Witt stood up straight, some of the dragon within him granting him courage. "I am a skald. And I am a villain. I have the power to save my people."

"And yet here you are and your people are not."

The icy patch grew, putting the fire to rest. "I can save them!" In his heart, he knew it was true. An idea formed of just how that might happen.

Vang laughed again. *"Do you know the difference between a dragon and a kobold, young one?"* When Witt didn't answer, the dragon continued. *"A dragon only looks out for itself. I can see a great power in you, one that yearns to be set free. But you will never be great while you attach yourself to those around you. If you want power, you must take it. Do not wait for it to be thrust upon you."*

Witt's mind raced. Dragons were no mere beast. They were smarter than most races, cunning and vile. If Vang discovered an inkling of what Witt intended, it would kill him in an instant.

Witt smiled. He no longer feared death. What he feared was a life without power. "May I play you a song?"

Vang curled back atop its pile of melted rubble. *"Carry on."*

Witt strummed his lute, letting the notes bounce off of the throne room walls. He played Inspired Frenzy, an ode to dragons and the birth of kobolds. As he sang, his gravelly voice blending with the music of his lute, Vang's eyes began to close. Next, he played Ballad of the Bold, but there were no heroes to benefit from its buff. He followed it with Song of Swiftness, and hot air swirled around his legs as the dragon's eyes drooped lower and lower. Song of Silence reduced the dragon's eyes to slits. By the time he finished Song of Enlightenment, gentle snores rocked the throne room.

In spite of the heat, a cool calmness coated Witt. He had lured Vang to sleep with his music, and now he would win it to his cause.

He plucked the strings slowly as he played Song of Seduction, and the words came out barely more than a whisper. With each pluck, red and pink smoke wafted out from the lute.

"The oldest songs, the oldest stories, they all detail one thing.
It's not of gold or glory, but of love and loss and pain.
For loving leads to laughter, and laughter leads to pain.
In love lies the storm, and no one escapes the rain."

As Witt continued to play, the colored smoke wafted out across the throne room, swirling and dancing with the music. It made its way to Vang and as it inhaled deeply in its slumber, the smoke disappeared in its fiery depths.

"Love has inspired kingdoms, and torn them to the ground.
It is a universal truth that happens all around.
Love has many faces, and also many truths.
Some love gold and power, and others love their youth.
Some love family, some love friends, some just love their self within.
But of all the ways to love, one stands above the rest.
The only way to truly love is—"

The throne room trembled as Vang shook. Smoke poured from its nostrils as it rose up, revealing the severity of its height. Its wings unfurled like giant sails flapping in the wind.

"Foolish kobold, do you think you can tame me with a spell meant for common beasts?" Vang roared, and fire poured forth like a furnace, melting the wall of the throne room. *"Do I look common to you?"*

Witt stepped back until his back hit the wall. "I—I uh—"

The dragon roared again, melting through the wall. The ceiling cracked and sagged where the wall had been, pieces of rubble crumbling to the ground.

Its jaws snapped shut and Vang cocked its head. *"Most interesting."*

Witt wasn't sure, but he thought the dragon's lip curled up in a smile.

"It seems we have a visitor. Another young one."

Witt's stomach dropped. *Kessy. It had to be her. But how had she gotten here so fast?*

"Ah, so you know her." Vang faced Witt, lowering its head until it was inches from his face. It took a deep sniff. *"More than that, you care for her."*

Vang returned to its perch atop the rubble, saying nothing. Witt could only assume it was talking to Kessy the same way that it had spoken to him.

Minutes passed slowly, and the only sounds were Witt's racing heart and the rumble of the dragon's heavy breathing.

A clop-clop echoed from outside the throne room, and a moment later Kessy entered the room riding Olah's boar. The boar fought to turn around, but Kessy urged it forward. She ignored Witt as her eyes fell upon the magnificent dragon.

Dragon and kobold gazed at one another, and Witt wondered what they could be saying.

Kessy climbed down from the boar and knelt in the same way Witt had. The boar snorted, and took off down the hallway.

Vang rolled its shoulders and lifted its head. Its eyes fell on Witt, and he had the sudden urge to run. He no longer felt safe in the dragon's presence.

Kessy fell out of her trance and turned to Witt. "Oh Witt! I'm so glad you're okay."

"Kessy, you need to lea—"

"Silence!" The walls of the throne room shook and the

sagging ceiling cracked further. *"You thought you could control me?"* Dark laughter echoed in Witt's mind. *"You want my power? It comes with a price."*

A chill coursed through Witt, but for once it wasn't calming. He had tried to toy with a dragon, and now he would suffer the consequences.

Vang paced about the throne room before stopping in front of Witt. Its long, reptilian neck descended until its nostrils flared inches from Witt's face. Heat radiated from its very being.

"You want to be a villain? You want true power? Then you must do what villains do." Vang turned to Kessy, taking a long drawn-out sniff before returning to its perch.

The kobold in Witt's vision pulsed.

"Witt, what's going on?" Concern radiated from her eyes. "What does it want?" The color had faded from her scales and she stood there frozen in fear.

Witt focused on the kobold image and his notifications appeared.

Notifications:

Quest: *Blood of the Dragon. As an emerging villain, you have dabbled with powers beyond your control. But the blood of the dragon runs through you, and a golden dragon has taken an interest in your quest. An alliance with dragons does not come cheap. For the destructive power of draconic flame, the golden dragon requires a sacrifice.*

Witt read the notification again and again. *The dragon requires a sacrifice. What could that possibly mean?*

"Witt," Kessy called again. "Let's get out of here. I don't like this."

He stepped toward her when Vang suddenly raised its head.

"Tell me, young one, would you sacrifice one to save many? Would you let go of what you hold most dear to achieve that which you most desire?"

Witt's gaze fell upon Kessy. She had been his oldest friend, and his biggest supporter for as far back as he could remember. She had come all the way to the mountain just to find him.

He knew what Vang wanted, but there was no way he could sacrifice her.

And yet he had already sacrificed one of his own. He'd sacrificed the elder kobold so that a young kobold might take his place. He'd done it for the greater good. What was Kessy's life compared to the power of a dragon?

Witt shook his head. *No, she is my friend.* If he sacrificed her, she would never respawn.

"Come on, Witt." She extended her hand to him. "Let's go."

He reached for her, but then let his hand fall. If he walked out of the throne room, he would never have the power he dreamed of. He would be committing to a life of servitude, where eventually he would lose all his villain points and become what he had always been, a skald who buffed heroes. He would fight it, but ultimately he would fail. Hux, Razul, Zirn, they would all die by his side. And so would Kessy.

His shoulders grew cold. He could never go back to that life. Kessy's essence would live on in the next kobold to hatch.

Witt strummed his lute and the colorful notes jumped toward Kessy.

Her face contorted. "Witt, what are you doing?"

She turned to run, but Witt started singing.

"In ancient times, when lands were young,
and dragons spoke the only tongue..."

A glaze overtook Kessy's eyes as his influence took hold, soon they began to glow red. He finished the song and she stood there, her scales pulsing with rage. Witt had complete control over her actions as he slowly marched her toward the dragon.

CHAPTER TWENTY

Witt held onto a crease between Vang's massive scales as they soared through the night sky. Heat radiated from the dragon's back, warming Witt as he sat with his legs spread at the base of its neck. They flew over mountains, and small fires flickered like fireflies from those camping below.

Further ahead, the glowing pyres of Skullheyden ignited the skull keep. Its ominous eyes followed them everywhere they went.

The warmth beneath him did nothing to melt the icy dread that filled Witt's insides.

He was no dragon. He was nothing more than cold rage and hatred. He had chosen his path and now nothing would stop him from achieving his goals.

If not for the heroes, he never would have fled to the mountain. He never would have forced Kessy to—

Witt closed his eyes, letting the night air assault his face. She was gone and there was nothing he could do to bring her back. There was no point in reliving those memories. The way she had—

He focused on Skullheyden. After tonight, everything would change.

"Relish this moment, young one. This will be but a taste of what you can achieve."

Witt let the anger consume him. He found it odd that in spite of everything, he held no animus toward Vang. Who was he to question a god? He'd tried to tame something that could not be tamed and Kessy had paid the price.

Kessy...

As much as he hated the heroes, he found that he hated himself just as much. He wasn't sure if there was a right or wrong choice. There was only a choice, and he had made his.

Vang tilted its head down and they began the descent. The fire pit in Murkwell was not burning for the first time in his memory. Were they all seeking safety in the burrows underneath?

He would check on them soon but first he had to send a message. To the heroes. To everyone. A message they would never forget.

Vang dove deep, pulling back at the last moment and letting its wings unfurl as it coasted high into the air. They billowed like sails, rocketing the golden creature high above Skullheyden's walls.

"Ready?" Vang invaded Witt's mind.

"Ready," Witt answered.

The city was quiet except for the flapping of the dragon's wings. Windows in the inns and houses glowed a dull yellow. The occasional vagabond or thief lurched around the city. Two guards stopped their patrol and pointed at the dragon. In a moment, they would set the alarm, but it would already be too late.

Witt's legs grew hot as the flying furnace he rode roared to life. Flames poured from Vang's mouth, setting The Merry Minotaur ablaze. The wooden beams ignited in an instant, and the flames leapt to the surrounding buildings. It only took seconds for the entire inn to collapse.

The kobold image in Witt's vision pulsed with activity as heroes met their doom. The Messy Unicorn Tavern was the next to go, followed by The Sour Turtle Inn, The Rusty Pickaxe Inn, The Singing Stag, and The Ghastly Dog Inn. They caught fire like a match to tinder.

Screams tore at the night. Fiery bodies ran into the streets and collapsed on the cobblestone. Witt felt no remorse.

Before the alarms had sounded, half of the inns and taverns sat in ruin. Dozens of heroes perished in the flames, and with their respawn point denied, there was no telling where they would end up.

As the flames brought the city to life, Witt's heart filled with ice.

He pulled up his notifications, watching the death toll rise.

Notifications:

You have killed a level 12 hero. X3
You have killed a level 9 hero. X2
You have killed a level 13 hero.
You have killed a level 8 hero. X5

The numbers ticked up by the second. As screams faded, the scroll unraveled longer and longer and his villain points continued to accumulate. He was sure there were many surprises in store for him.

The world beneath him burned. Vang hovered in the air,

violent fire spewing from its mouth burning shops and homes.

As smoke filled the air, blocking his vision of the carnage, Witt couldn't help but think that maybe Kessy's death had been for something.

There was no longer a path for Witt to follow. The time had come to forge his own.

He took a final look at the burning city, then he and Vang disappeared into the night.

EPILOGUE

The moon shined bright overhead, casting the throne room of The Cursed Catacombs in a silver glow. Witt sat on a throne carved from melted rock, his lute draped across his legs. Vang lay curled up on the rubble behind him, its snores shaking the room with each exhale.

A pebble fell from the hole in the mountain above. It clattered against the stone floor, coming to stop at Witt's feet.

"Can't you use the entrance like a normal kobold?" Witt turned his gaze upward.

Razul leapt down from the opening, landing with a soft thud. He eyed the sleeping dragon before flashing Witt a smile. "Where's the fun in that?"

"What news do you have for me tonight?"

Razul came closer, taking a seat on a large piece of the crumbled ceiling. "Rumors, nothing more."

"And what of these rumors?" Witt's gaze bored into the rogue.

"Your reputation continues to grow. Heroes from far lands have begun the journey to claim the bounty on your head." He smirked. "Long live The Kobold King."

Let them try. No one has made it past the second level of The Cursed Catacombs, and with each new death, my dungeon grows stronger.

Witt stroked his chin. "Find out what you can about these new heroes. Inform Zirn, and make sure he makes the proper arrangements."

Razul nodded, and with a small bow, he disappeared into the hallway.

Witt leaned back against his throne. He'd made a formidable fortress within Corvin Mountain. After his rampage through Skullheyden, he'd been able to lay claim to the dungeon. Now, it was filled with fearsome monsters, cunning kobolds, and traps beyond measure. Every day it grew stronger. His people were safe and protected within its quarters.

Many an angry hero had come looking for vengeance. All had failed.

Vang stirred behind Witt. *"Interesting."* Its voice invaded his mind. *"We have a visitor."*

Witt shrugged. "What of it? The dungeon grows stronger by the day. They've barely even scratched the surface of what we have in store."

"This one comes bearing a gift."

Witt activated Dungeon Vision and found himself looking through the eyes of a kobold guard. He peered through the slat in the enchanted door Zirn had installed. A human clad in all black waited on the other side. A cowl concealed the stranger's face.

Witt took control of the kobold's body. "The dungeon is closed until the break of dawn. What do you want?"

The stranger lifted a hand and showed a rope that disappeared behind his body. "I come with an offering for The Kobold King."

He jerked on the rope and a dwarf stumbled forward. Rope bound his hands, arms, chest, and mouth.

Witt's heart pounded in his ears and for a moment he lost track of what the stranger was saying. His focus was on Stu. The silver clasps in the dwarf's red beard clinked as he struggled to speak.

A pleasant chill ran down Witt's spine as he opened the door, allowing the stranger entry.

Witt instructed the guard to escort them to the throne room and returned to his own body. His hands shook with malevolence. With his newfound abilities, he'd put a bounty on Stu's head. For weeks, the dwarf had remained hidden. However, the stranger had managed to do what others could not.

He paced around the room, Vang's eyes following his movement. When he heard the patter of feet from down the hall, Witt returned to his throne.

The guard waited at the door and the stranger entered pulling the dwarf behind him. Stu's eyes spread wide when he laid eyes on Witt. He struggled to run, but the stranger pulled him back, kicking the dwarf behind the knees and forcing him to kneel.

The stranger then knelt beside the dwarf, and lowered his head.

"Stand," ordered Witt. "Stand, and reveal yourself so that you may claim your reward."

The stranger stood. "This is not a claim for bounty. I desire more than that."

Vang lifted its head, and the stranger stepped back.

"Careful, stranger." Witt leaned forward. "You do not make demands of a king."

The stranger bowed. "You are right. I meant no offense." He tossed the rope that bound Stu in front of him. "This is a gift."

The stranger removed his cowl, revealing a plain face with a scar under the right eye. He was the bandit Witt had spared the night they ambushed the caravan. "I have paid my dues, and I wish to join your cause."

"So it begins." Vang rose to its feet, stepping down from the mound of rubble and sniffing the bandit. The bandit kept his eyes focused on Witt. *"He speaks the truth."*

Witt nodded. "Very well. I think we may find use for your talents." He turned to the guard. "Take the dwarf to the cells. I will deal with him later. When you are done, send a message to Razul. I have found him an apprentice."

Stu's screams lingered in Witt's mind. They comforted him in a way nothing else had. Midway through, the dwarf's eyes had gone vacant. It didn't matter though, Witt had still had his fun.

As he made his way back to the throne room, Vang invaded his mind once again. *"There is something you should see."*

Witt called back to the dragon but received no response. He quickened his pace, climbing stairs as fast as he could.

In the throne room, Hux, Mido, and two guards stood beside a short paladin wearing red armor. A burlap sack concealed the hero's features. Witt scowled. What importance could a gnome or halfling have that was worth bringing them before him?

Hux bowed to Witt as he entered. "This one tried to complete the dungeon alone. We halted our attacks, and barred the gate as soon as we realized what she was."

Witt frowned, anger rising up inside of him. "What does it matter what she is? She's a hero. They can all rot in the catacombs."

Vang laughed, its deep voice shaking the throne room.

"What's so funny?" Witt snapped. He had no time for games with heroes.

"I think you should see for yourself." Hux removed the sack from the paladin's head.

A reptilian face looked at Witt. Dark-black scales faded to red around her snout, and two ivory horns jutted upwards just behind her ears.

"My lord." The kobold paladin nodded, unable to move anything else due to the guards holding her in place. "I have come in search of a quest."

Witt stared at the kobold hero before him, a smile creeping at the edge of his face. "I may have a task..."

ACKNOWLEDGMENTS

Thank you, dear reader, for checking out Path to Villainy. What began as a simple attempt to take my mind off of the chaos of 2020 quickly morphed in the book you're holding right now. Watching Witt transform from a doe-eyed kobold to unapologetic villain was some of the most fun I've had in my writing career. If you would like to see more of Witt and his path to villainy, make sure to leave a review. Reviews are the lifeblood of indie authors like myself and help provide social proof that this story is worth taking a chance on.

Many people had a hand in the creation of this book, so sit back while I roll the credits.

Thank you to Scotty for being an incredible friend throughout all of this, not just with Path to Villainy, but with everything that has happened this year. Here's to many more nights of fun and gaming.

Cindy, just like with every other story, you have helped give these characters their beating hearts and emotional depth.

Thank you to my Patreon supporters who continue to

believe and support me even when I'm writing slow and behind schedule. Tim Krason, Michael Percell, Eric Sprague, Heather Jarvis, Jesse Frazel, Robert Schaefer, Frank Pisauro, Lawrence Novak, Rickie Brookes.

Thank you to my beta readers: Tony Gallo, Bri Bish, Steven Gene Mills, Garith Ro, John Vann, Brandon Pyatt, Dennis Heizelman, Ozzie Azuna.

I owe a great deal to everyone in S.L. Rowland's Secret Society for the character names and direction of this story.

Anthony Westenberg for naming "Whit" who eventually became "Witt."

Bill Shupe who suggested Witt's class be a skald.

Bri Bish for naming "Cerent" and also suggesting Kobold as the race.

James Miller and John Smith for suggesting an evil plot-line or evil MC.

Michael Percell for naming "Schekt."

Asher James Rickard for naming the dragon "Vang."

Tim Parkinson, for Vang's title "The Undying."

If you're looking for more books similar to my own, check out the Gamelit Society and LitRPG Books, two of the best places for all things Gamelit and LitRPG. Thank again!

Until next time...

ABOUT THE AUTHOR

S.L. Rowland is a nomad. Born in the South, he loves traveling and has road-tripped coast to coast three times over. He currently lives in St. Louis with his Shiba Inu, Lawson. When not writing, he enjoys hiking, reading, weightlifting, playing video games and having his heart broken by various Atlanta sports teams.

SLRowland.com

S.L. Rowland's Secret Society

Email: slrowland@slrowland.com

Sign up for S.L. Rowland's Mailing List for updates on new releases, short stories and all things *S.L. Rowland* related!

ALSO BY S.L. ROWLAND

Sentenced to Troll

Sentenced to Troll 2

Sentenced to Troll 3

Pangea Online: Death and Axes

Pangea Online: Magic and Mayhem

Vestiges: Portal to The Apocalypse

60400956R00106